FAMILY REUNION . . .

Meltrope and her fellow archers walked us to a small room off the courtyard. And there . . . I spoke with my mother for the first time in ten years.

"So. You came," she said.

"I wasn't given much choice."

"Yes, I know. Loki's efforts did not go unnoticed. But you escaped. I'm sure there's a story there. Loki is very dangerous, very clever . . . for a god."

At that point the conversation ground to a halt. This was it? We were to stand awkwardly in a musty little room, sounding like strangers who strike up a desultory conversation while waiting for a bus?

"How have you been, Senda?"

"I go by Senna now," I said.

She frowned. "Senna? That's the name of a tree. The bark is used for medicines. Mostly for laxatives.

"Yes. Fortunately the kids at school don't spend a lot of time reading dictionaries."

She looked down at the floor. "How have you been?"

"How have I been? For the last ten years after you dumped me off? How have I been, the only one like me stuck in a world full of deaf, dumb, and blind fools? Fine, Mom. Fine. How have you been?!"

Look for other EVERWORLD titles

by K.A. Applegate:

#1 Search for Senna
#2 Land of Loss
#3 Enter the Enchanted
#4 Realm of the Reaper
#5 Discover the Destroyer
#6 Fear the Fantastic
#7 Gateway to the Gods
#8 Brave the Betrayal

EVER WORLD

INSIDE THE ILLUSION

K.A. APPLEGATE

SCHOLASTIC INC.
New York Toronto London Auckland Sydney
Mexico City New Delhi Hong Kong

ISBN 0-590-87855-7

12 11 10 9 8 7 6 5 4 3 2 1 0/0 1 2 3 4 5/0

Printed in the U.S.A.

First Scholastic printing, September 2000

For Michael and Jake

Inside the Illusion

I was seven years old when my mother told me she was going away.

I remember the lights on the train were too bright; they made it impossible to see out of the windows. The car jerked and bumped. A man slept, chin down on his chest, wheezing. A nurse had taken off one white shoe and was rubbing her foot.

We sat on hard plastic seats, my mother and I. She was nervous, jumpy, I could tell that much. She looked too closely at the other passengers. She whispered to me, putting her lips right against my ear, tickling.

"I know you don't understand, Senda. You can't understand, not really, not now. But if I keep you, honey, if we stay together, it will cause trouble. Bad people might . . . I don't want to scare you, sweetie, I don't want you to worry. You just have to trust your mommy. Someday you'll know." She put her hand against my cheek, stroked my cheek and hair. Kissed the side of my head.

"Where are you going?" I asked. I had no idea, of course, I was too little. No idea that this night would be the last I saw of her.

"Mommy has to go far away, to a very different kind of place. Mommy has to leave. She's sorry, I'm so sorry, I never should have . . . but someday maybe you'll leave, too, Senda. Maybe, I hope not, I really do, I hope you'll find a way to be okay, to be normal. Oh, sweetie."

She talked on and on, a loop, repetitive, meandering, filling time and space with words that meant nothing to me.

I watched the other people on the train. None of them glowed. None of them shone with the pale light that I saw around my mother. None of them was like us. No one ever was. There was only us, I knew that, had known it forever, it seemed. Only we were like us. A minority of two.

That night I met my father for the first time. I had my little suitcase and a Barbie backpack. I had my few toys, my clothes, my books. We emerged from the CTA station and stepped into a canyon of overpoweringly tall buildings. I knew what this place was called, it was "downtown."

It was late, dark. The streets weren't deserted — Chicago streets are never entirely deserted — but there was an empty, depopulated feeling.

Yellow cabs glided past, their "available" lights glowing. Limousines splashed through puddles of recent rain. An occasional bus would gasp and struggle by, leaving an oily smell in its wake.

Pedestrians were few. They walked fast and kept their faces buried in collars and scarves. It was cold, wet cold. Across the street an Italian restaurant with a gaudy red, green, and white marquee. A Kinko's, wide-awake and bright white, but empty aside from a long-haired guy standing over a massive copier, eyes glazed, head bobbing to music I didn't hear.

I looked up. The buildings rose forever, up into a sky of orange-tinted darkness. The stars were washed away by the lights, the moon invisible.

"Come on," she said, and we crossed at the light. She held my hand, she carried my little suitcase, and I carried my Barbie pack. I didn't like it, I didn't like Barbie, but it was mine, and having it with me helped.

We pushed our way through a heavy glass door into a half-lit mausoleum of a lobby, all granite and brushed aluminum and recessed lights. A guard looked up, surprised to see the likes of us.

"We're here to see Tom O'Brien," my mother said.

The guard made a phone call. Then we got on the elevator and rode it up and up, neither of us speaking. Music was playing. The elevator dinged as we passed each floor.

We rode all the way alone. We stopped and found ourselves in another lobby, more carpet and walnut. The lights were low here, too. I heard someone typing on a keyboard. Saw a man in a white shirt down one hallway. He was talking to someone inside an office. He looked excited.

From the other direction came a tall man. He seemed so old to me. He had gray hair on the sides of his head, a worried look, lines in his forehead. But his eyes were soft as he looked at me.

"Anica, what are you doing?" he asked my mother.

"I have no choice, Tom. She's your daughter. I can't keep her. If I do, we'll both be in danger. You have no concept . . . no idea."

He drew her away, looked back over his shoulder, and said, "Stay right there. Don't go anywhere."

He ushered her into an office and closed the

door. I went and listened. Crouched and pressed my ear to the fine, satin-finished walnut.

". . . crazy? You can't just come waltzing in here and drop off a little girl. I have a family. I have a wife and a daughter of my own."

"You had a wife when you were having me," she said sharply.

"Yes, and it was wrong, and if I'd known you had a baby I'd have helped with support. But you took off. You never told me. You —"

"There's no time for all this," my mother interrupted wearily. "Come. Take my hand."

Even through the door I could feel it, the glow. That's what I called it, the glow, that's what my mother taught me to call it. A light that shines from nowhere, a light that people can't see. I felt her take the glow within her, focus it, direct it, use it. It all passed through me, that glow; we were one and inseparable, my mother and I, united by the glow.

There was a pause. Then my mother's voice again, softer, soothing. "Now it's all better, isn't it? You're a good man, Tom. You want to do what's right. You want to live up to your responsibilities."

No answer at first. Then a vague, troubled voice. "Yes. Of course."

"You still love me."

"Yes." Not a ringing affirmation, more of a reluctant confession.

"You'll take her. For me."

"I . . ."

"My will is your will, Tom. My needs, your needs. Your worries will come to nothing. All will be well. All is well. You will take the girl, you will raise her, protect her, keep her as safe as it is within your power to do."

"Yes," the man said. A sleepwalker mumbling.

"Good. Remember." Then, in a different, more businesslike tone, she said, "Don't worry, Tom, you won't have her for long. The powers will find her or she will find them."

"Anica, I don't understand. . . ."

"No. But she will. Someday. She's listening now. She's outside the door, I can feel her there."

I jerked away from the door, face burning. But then I decided to listen again. What harm would there be? My mother was leaving me. What could she do that was worse than that?

And then she was speaking to me, right through the door, as if she could see me, as if she had heard my bitter, unvoiced question.

"You are great and dangerous, Senda. I named you 'pathway' but may you never become one. If we stay together, the two of us together in one place . . . too dangerous, and I am too weak, Senda, my innocent little girl. But the day may come, forbid! But if the day comes, look for me with Mother Isis."

"What did you say her name was?" my father asked.

"Senda. My lovely daughter, Senda, the Pathway."

"Senna?" he repeated, losing the soft Spanish "d" sound in his flat Midwestern pronunciation.

And from that day, I was Senna. I was his daughter. And I knew that I was different.

My mother never came out of the office. I heard my father gasp. I felt a terrific rush of power, the glow, unfiltered. And a few moments later my father emerged, white as a ghost, shaking.

I looked inside. My mother was gone.

CHAPTER II

"Hey, witchy woman," Christopher said, pitching his voice to be overheard by everyone. "Hey, hey, witchy woman? Are you sure you can't make a six-pack of Heinies appear? I mean, you can move a whole freaking river and you can't work up a six-pack? It's okay if it's cans. I'm not saying it has to be bottles."

I ignored him. As a rule I ignore all of them. They hate me. They blame me. They're afraid of me. All of which means very little to me. What matters to me is the question of whether they do as I need them to do. Humans aren't chess pieces, they do after all have free will — to some degree — but a good player can still use them.

In fact, playing humans is harder. Or maybe I should say it simply requires different skills. A chess grandmaster has to be able to see his own and his opponent's moves, six or seven plays into the future. That's impossible with humans, of course. Humans are pawns or bishops or rooks who may on occasion move in impossible ways.

Chess pieces don't do that. The knight does not simply decide to move two spaces forward and three back.

To play humans you need less of an ability to see many moves ahead, more of an ability to adapt swiftly, to keep your eye on one or more goals simultaneously, and to be prepared to add human free will into your own equation.

"Heineken?" April said, just to make conversation and annoy me. "I would never have thought of you as an imported-beer kind of guy, Christopher."

"Well, I'm not saying I would turn down a humble Budweiser. I just thought, hey, if the Wicked Witch of the North Shore can do it, why not go upmarket?"

Thus far in Everworld I had managed to escape Loki, escape Merlin, and weaken Huitzilopoctli, which in turn weakened Ka Anor. Of course there had been failures, too. I had failed to use Hel for my own ends. That was overreaching on my part. Hel is just a mad beast; I should have realized that.

Worse yet, I had lost control of David. Not all

control — he would always want me, always love me, always have to fight the urge to think first of my needs and demands. But that bitch Athena . . .

"Guinness," April said. "That's beer. Or stout, I guess they call it."

Well, live and learn. Live and learn and grow stronger. I could feel it. Every day I was stronger. Every day the force that ran through Everworld like electricity through a live wire was easier for me to reach, to touch, to manipulate. I could see lines of power everywhere, sense them, draw their power into me. Use them.

And more than use them, feed on them. Normal people would never know the pleasure. They would never know how empty their lives were without the glow. Even I had only seen a part of it in the old days, the days of my long exile in the real world. There the glow is a mere trickle coming through the rift between universes. There the glow touched me and I touched it, but it was a weak, paltry light that only kept my soul from freezing but never made me warm.

Here, ah, this was the source. I had been Neptune, Pluto, out in the cosmic darkness squinting to see a far-distant star. Here I stood in the full tropical glare of that sun. The light was everywhere. The light was within me. No longer a glow, but a furnace.

Could I make a six-pack of beer appear? No. Make what did not exist suddenly exist? Of course not, even most gods can't do that. And I am no god, but a mere mortal with unusual abilities.

Still, I had tapped into the deep powers and moved a river.

The memory filled me up, rushed through me, the sensation of power more erotic than any fantasy, more exciting. My skin crawled and tingled with it. I could scream from the pleasure of all that magic, all that light flowing into me, through me.

"Look," David said. "See something shining up there? Is that a river?"

"God, I hope so," Christopher said. "I am running out of sweat."

We paused atop a scruffy knoll and they all shaded their eyes and blinked in the blinding sun, trying to see clearly. I closed my eyes and saw more clearly than any of them. Oh yes, it was a river. A river that vibrated with energy. *The* river.

"Looks like a river, those are clearly trees, some kind of a valley," Jalil said. "Although with this heat the water could be an illusion, a mirage."

"Can't you tell for sure, Spock?" Christopher mocked. "Spock, we count on you."

"It's the Nile," I said with quiet satisfaction.

"It speaks!"

"You're sure?" David asked.

"Follow that river downstream and we will be in Egypt," I said.

Yes, soon in Egypt. Would my mother be surprised to see me? Probably not. She had known or at least suspected that this time would come. Would she be afraid? That was the question.

I had told Athena that my mother was more powerful than I. Was that true? Was it too soon to force a test?

No choice but to trust my instincts. And my experience. I had learned to be a judge of powers. I had learned the hard way not to provoke the gods. And I knew that even now Merlin was greater than I. That old man was a power, yes he was, though I would still see him burned down.

But my mother? What might she have learned in the service of Isis?

I smothered the growing nervousness, drew my mind away from fear. It was too late to turn back now. I had not intended to go to Egypt so soon, but the occasion had arisen, and chess player that I am, I had to exploit the moment. At least it had gotten me away from Olympus.

We had a long way to go to reach the river. At least another four hours across more hot sand with little shelter from the blistering sun. And with too little water. But I could not complain or show any weakness. They had to continue to think of me as nearly invulnerable. They could whine and complain, I could not.

I was faint, dragging, eyes bleary by the time we reached the green belt that ran along both banks of the river and made the shallow valley a near paradise. And now we had shade beneath waving date palms and orange trees. No water, but the oranges were ripe and we picked them, split them open to find bloodred pulp that gushed with sticky-sweet juice.

"These are killer oranges," Jalil said.

"No pesticides, no hormones, totally organic and tree-ripened," April said with satisfaction.

"Yeah, well, don't spend all your time eating," David muttered.

Out of the open spaces and surrounded by widely spaced trees, David became more cautious. He has the true military instinct; he knew the trees could hide enemies. He loosened the sword of Galahad and said very little, watching, watching all the while.

I had chosen well with him. He was a victim of his own male insecurities, a prisoner of every honor-duty-sacrifice masculine myth. Very useful.

My hook was still in him. But it was his core character that I relied on. He hated himself, David did. Hated himself for failing as a child to resist molestation. He would never let himself up off the floor for that. He would demand ever-greater evidence that he was a man, a man, a capital *M* man. He would never, ever find satisfaction.

And he would never truly turn against me, never really abandon me, he couldn't. He had to be the hero or die trying.

My half sister, April, began to sing. A perky little melody from some no-doubt popular singer. April likes to sing. She's a showy, superficial person. She wants to be an actress and may well accomplish that minor goal — and no more.

She was the daughter in my father's house, the one and only, the adored, cute, perky, sweet-faced, red-haired, Talbot-Kids-wearing girl, the beloved one, when I moved in with my Barbie backpack and nouveau-bohemian clothes.

It was contempt at first sight. I've never liked her. On her good days she amused me. On her bad days I found her self-righteous religiosity, her smug normalcy intolerable.

Christopher began to babble under the reviving influence of the oranges, an oversized kid on a sugar rush. "Hey, maybe this isn't Egypt. Maybe it's Florida. Keep a sharp eye out for old people.

Anyone spots a golf course where all the players are ninety years old, we've gone right past Egypt and ended up in Lauderdale."

Originally I had chosen Christopher because of his weaknesses. He would keep David off-guard, he would be an irritant, never let the group truly coalesce. A lightweight bigot, an alcoholic, a selfish coward. But Christopher was maturing and causing less dissension than I had hoped.

Pity. I would have to see what I could do about making beer. Maybe I could drown the reborn, new-and-improved Christopher in alcohol.

For now, though, there actually seemed to be a friendship growing between Christopher and Jalil. Evidence of the unpredictability of human chess pieces.

Jalil had been a major disappointment, greater even than Christopher. I thought I had him. But my hold over Jalil was a bluff now, and he knew it.

Jalil is a very intelligent young man with a twisted brain. Obsessive-compulsive, a hand washer, a counter, a person ruled by uncontrollable, irrational impulses that are the distorted mirror of his own cold rationalism. He will stand at a sink washing and washing till his skin cracks and bleeds and he cries, sobs, unable to resist.

But for some reason I didn't understand, the compulsions were absent from the Everworld Jalil.

That weakened my hold. That and the fact that Jalil suffers from the vice of stubbornness. He is not easily bluffed or intimidated. I misjudged him. Underestimated him. He was a hard piece to play.

I had chosen David to play the soldier, Christopher to play the clown, April to play the peacemaker. And I had chosen Jalil to be the scientist. Because I could never rule safely till I had my hands on the software, as Jalil called it.

I loved the glow, needed it. I was filled with it. But I was never a mystic like my mother. I was never content to let it be, let it flow. I was a child of the twenty-first century, not some fugitive from the Dark Ages like her. I didn't want mumbo jumbo and Wiccan spirituality, I wanted control.

I needed to understand the software. I needed the codes, and to be able to rewrite them. And Jalil would die trying to find those codes. He can't help himself any more than David can.

That should have been enough, but now Jalil was becoming dangerous. He'd shown that in our passage through Africa. He had tried to use me, had used me, and had even forced David to help him.

I suppressed a shudder, clenched my jaw tight to keep from screaming. The smug bastard had used me!

No, no, just embarrassing or manipulating Jalil was no longer nearly enough. Jalil had used me. I would hear his screams for that. I would watch his agony and laugh.

Not that I would enjoy it. I was not a sadist. But I had a destiny. Nothing could be allowed to get in the way of that, surely that was obvious. It should have been obvious to Jalil.

Did he think I resisted Loki's attempt to use me, Merlin's attempt to use me, everyone's attempt to turn me into their own personal little turnstile, making me an object, depriving me of control, of power? Did he really think I would let him use me and not make him suffer, not make him plead for mercy, not make him scream till his filthy throat was raw?

I could do it right now. I had moved a river. I could do it right now, couldn't I?

I watched him, stared at the back of his neck, he was ahead of me, watched his scrawny form move in dappled sunlight, watched him gnaw at a split orange, and thought, *Shall I kill you now, Jalil?* I felt anticipation within me. Felt the stirring of the carnal lust that filled me with every use of the great power.

No. No, what if I tried and failed? What if I failed?

Why didn't he wash his hands? Where had his

weakness gone? Was it a by-product of the cross-universe shift? Or was he protected?

Ah, that was the question. That is what stayed my hand. Had someone, some power, some god, seen my scheme and made just the subtle changes needed to weaken me?

Was I someone else's chess piece?

We reached the river without incident. An accomplishment in Everworld, where no innocent walk is ever free of mortal danger.

The river was broad, slow, almost sluggish. Too wide, too slow.

Of course I saw a different river than the others did. They saw indifferent, opaque, silt-choked water. I saw the bright glow of enchantment, the sense of a thing vibrating, like a plucked violin string.

And yet, up close it felt wrong. I sensed frustration of purpose. A certain strangeness, resentment, energy penned and controlled, energy that wanted release.

Something was wrong. I almost told David. I glanced at him. He had not noticed. His senses did not extend beyond the usual boundaries of human limitations. He saw only visible light and felt nothing of magic.

Jalil noticed what David and I had both missed: the purely physical facts.

"Look at the water level. Look at the trees over there."

A stand of palms was growing out of the water. Looking back up the riverbank, I saw other examples. Trees that had clearly been flooded. The river was out of its banks.

"It's normal," Jalil went on. "The Nile floods every year. Supposed to happen, you know, it deposits silt and all. But this doesn't feel like a flood to me. See, look how those trees are rotting. You can see they're dying. Which means this water's been too high for too long. Floods should come and go in a couple of weeks, maybe. See, look at those reeds, all kinds of them growing, and that shouldn't be if the water had just flooded and was going down."

"I'm telling you, this young man has not fallen asleep in class ever," Christopher said, pointing at Jalil as if he were the prize freak on display. "Let me ask you something, Jalil: When you go online in the library, you actually do research instead of downloading pictures of naked cheerleaders, don't you? You're a very disturbed young man."

"What is it with guys and cheerleaders?" April muttered.

Jalil shrugged and with false humility said, "Well, anyway, what do I know? I'm not a geologist or a botanist."

"It stinks," April observed. "Smells kind of rotten. Like dead fish."

"We continue heading downstream, I assume?" David asked me.

"Yes."

He peered closely at me, seeking to penetrate. But that's not his specialty. All he could do was stare at me with his big innocent eyes and hope I would take pity. I did.

"I would be cautious," I said. "Something is wrong."

"Ah, it speaks again," Christopher mocked. "She delivers up another fortune cookie. That would be your magic powers at work, huh, Senna? There's something wrong every three freaking steps in this big outdoor Home for the Crazy-assed. Wow, thanks for that heads-up."

I ignored him. There was no other way. To engage in back-and-forth would only diminish me and would do nothing to lessen their hostility.

"Let's get a drink, fill our waterskins, cool off for half an hour, and then we'll saddle up again and get moving." David made the suggestion, but it sounded like an order.

Jalil was gazing back the way we had come. "I guess the Coo-Hatch are —"

David cut him off with a look. Jalil nodded imperceptibly. He was annoyed. David had silenced him and done it too crudely.

Something was going on. Or had gone on. Something involving David and Jalil and the Coo-Hatch.

"They saved us once," David said, elaborately casual. "I imagine they'll do it again, if they can. It's nice having backup but it would be better if I knew how much. I can't get a clear view of them. I never see more than one of the Tinkerbells and maybe an impression of one or two Grouchos."

I resisted the urge to roll my eyes. The Coo-Hatch were an alien species. The adult Coo-Hatch looked like odd, flightless birds, twisted into the shape of a letter *C*. They walked with an odd shuffle that my companions insisted on describing as a Groucho walk. Their juvenile form was far smaller, fast, and flew with sudden, jerky acceleration. Thus "Tinkerbell."

The Coo-Hatch were following us in hopes of reaching my mother alive. The Coo-Hatch had been kidnapped to Everworld by their own gods. After a century marooned, wandering the face of

Everworld in small nomadic bands, they wanted to go home. They wanted me to be a gateway for them, to open the pathway between their universe and this one.

I was a very wanted woman. It almost might have been flattering.

I had convinced Athena, and by extension the Coo-Hatch, that I lacked that power, since the Coo-Hatch universe is different from my own. I convinced the goddess of wisdom that my mother could do it. She could release the Coo-Hatch, and the Coo-Hatch would then reward Athena by ending their cooperation with the Hetwan.

All of which, not coincidentally, helped me as well. The Coo-Hatch were a danger to Athena because the Coo-Hatch had learned to make guns. They were a danger to me for the same reason. Magic does not trump technology — a fact I was counting on.

But now Jalil and David shared a secret. Not a terrible dark secret, I guessed, but something. Something about the Coo-Hatch.

Wheels within wheels. Everworld is a very political place. But interestingly so. No one fights over tax rates. They fight over survival rates. It was a great big stew of intrigue, backstabbing, murder, and terror. It made me laugh, and April shot a suspicious look at me.

"Daydreaming?" she asked me.

"Remembering," I answered. "Remembering the time when I first came to live with you. You were so warm and welcoming. Such a good little soldier trying to make the best of a bad situation. You loaned me one of your stuffed animals to sleep with. I used to cry myself to sleep hugging that little panda bear."

For about three seconds April bought it. Her hard gaze flickered, confused. The set line of her mouth softened. Then . . . one, two, three . . . she remembered.

"It was a Tigger. Not a panda bear."

I laughed and was rewarded by the red flush in her cheeks. It was a good idea to poke each of them with a sharp stick every now and then, keep them off-balance. April would now spend the next hour stewing, seething.

Hatred is a weak force — it saps people, disturbs their thinking, twists their perspectives. Makes them forget their larger goals. April had started by wanting merely to get back to what she insists on calling the real world. But now April had been drawn into Everworld's grip. In part by her hatred of me.

They were so easy sometimes.

We washed in the river. April went downstream, I went upstream. The guys stayed in the middle. I was shielded from view by a patch of berry bushes. I didn't recognize the berries but I believe I may have the power to transmute most poisons. I took a chance and ate one. It was delicious. I stuffed more into my mouth, greedy. I was hungry but it was part of my mystique that I ate very little. A small part of my campaign of intimidation.

I undressed and waded into the river. Oh, yes, something was wrong here. I could feel it so clearly now that I was in direct contact with the water, now that its warmth flowed over my skin.

Frustration. The waters were frustrated. I felt their discomfort as I would have felt the embarrassment of a stutterer who can't get a word out. The waters were trying and failing to do as they had been charged.

Something else, too. Something more personal. A feeling of hostility. Not the river. Someone . . . Danger!

I saw nothing but a ripple. I leaped back, windmilling my arms, off balance, fell, submerged. The crocodile snapped and missed. Jaws that could crush a human skull like a fist crushing a kiwi fruit snapped so close to my head that I smelled the beast's carrion breath.

I kicked, my feet dug mud, no traction, backswam, pushed the water with frantic arms, and the monster surged, green-gray snout surmounted by murderous yellow eyes.

The mouth was all pink and puffy, lined with jagged teeth in swollen gums. I couldn't move, couldn't get up, the water was fighting me, the mud sucked at my limbs, my hand was in it now, sunk in mud, like quicksand. The crocodile couldn't miss me, not this time.

Did I have the power? I commanded the mud to release me. Ordered the waters to wash the monster away. Nothing, nothing but faint, derisive laughter beneath the level of true hearing.

The power would not come to me, would not reach me. I was cut off!

In slow motion all the universe was converging on this one place, this one point, all reality collapsing to this one event. I saw my left leg within the creature's mouth. My pitifully thin calf, scarred by too many walks in too many harsh places, lay on display, helpless, on a bed of rotting flesh and razor teeth.

The crocodile waited, jaw open. Waited, like it wanted me to try and jerk away. Like it was playing with me. Me the mouse and it the cat.

I froze. Returned the creature's stare. Helpless, helpless as any mortal. I could die. I could die right here, right now, a bloody, horrifying death.

And now they were all around me, whipping

the muddy water to dirty foam, a dozen or more crocodiles, all around me, surrounding me, taking an arm, a leg, a hand, a thigh. And all waited, all waited as I felt my heart stop beating in terror.

A signal. They awaited a signal. Then they would all close their jaws at once and I would be ripped apart, dismembered; bloody bits of Senna Wales would fill the stomachs of a dozen monsters.

My blood would stain the waters of the Nile and bring a message to my mother that she no longer had me to fear.

Voices. The others rushing up, breathless. David in the lead. They stood above me, gaped down like stunned baboons.

I made quite a sight. I lay there naked and mud-smeared and terrified, my entire body supported on the lower jaws of an army of crocodiles.

"Freeze!" David snapped. "No one move."

At least he knew not to go charging in. At least he understood that he was not faster than a closing jaw. He was helpless. All he could do was provoke.

By all the demons of all the underworlds, I hated him then. Hated Jalil and April as they gloated at my helplessness. Yes, they gloated, yes, they laughed inside, laughed themselves sick at me, though they hid it behind masks of shock and horror.

"What the hell is this about?!" Christopher demanded, sounding frightened.

"Senna, don't move," April cried.

The stupid cow. As if I didn't understand. As if I didn't know I was in danger.

"Not exactly a naturally occurring part of alligator life, I'm guessing," Jalil said. "There has to be a god involved."

"We serve the Lord Sobek," one of the crocodiles said.

"Talking alligators," Christopher muttered. "Of course. Why wouldn't they be talking alligators?"

"Shut up, you stupid fools," I raged. I felt a hundred teeth pressing into arm and leg and back, thigh and neck. I lay on a bed of nails, my weight distributed across all those ivory points. One wrong move, one twitch, and skin would tear and blood would gush. My head rested inside a mouth that could come down with such sudden force that my eyes would pop from their sockets, my brain . . .

"Hey, I have an idea," Christopher shot back. "Let's all take a walk. Let the gators enjoy their chicken leg lunch."

I tried to recover my shattered confidence. I

was seconds away from death. I could feel death in its thousand faces all crowding close to me. I could feel the hot breath of demons on me as they floated up from beneath the ground, beneath the water, peeked up at me from their foul underworld kingdoms.

Had to ignore all that. Had to focus on the true danger. This god Sobek held the key, that was obvious, but what was he? I knew the names of only a handful of the Egyptian gods. They were fluid in nature. They melded into one another, without fixed personalities or attributes. They were impossible to learn.

"Great and glorious Lord Sobek," I cried, struggling to keep the tears out of my voice. It couldn't end here. It couldn't end like this. This was to be my universe. Everworld was mine; it couldn't end like this.

"Great and glorious Lord Sobek, hear my pleas," I repeated.

"No, no, no," a deep, angry voice muttered, the sound bubbling up from beneath me, up through the water to become a muffled gurgle. "That is not the correct form of entreaty. I cannot reply to an appeal that is entirely wrong in form."

"What the hell?" David wondered.

"How shall I address you?" I asked the unseen

god. I was staring up at a sickened, drowned palm tree. The tree, the sky, and the curve of the crocodile's upper jaw. I couldn't look around, couldn't move. Stinking carnivore breath nearly gagged me.

"I am Lord Sobek, god of the crocodiles of the Nile, called Rager, son of Seth and his consort Neith, called the nurse of crocodiles."

I tried to get my frozen brain to work. What was it he wanted? "Lord Sobek, god of alligators of —"

"No, no, no! Alligators?" the god snapped impatiently. "You can hardly beg for my mercy if you cannot even call upon me in the proper form."

"I don't . . ." I said, desperate, losing my breath.

Jalil said, "Lord Sobek, god of the crocodiles of the Nile, called Rager, son of Seth and his consort Neith, nurse of crocodiles."

"Yes, mortal," the voice said, all calm reason now.

I felt the waters churn and slowly he rose into my view. He had the body of a man, bare from the waist upward. Or god, since he was at least seven feet tall. But his head was a crocodile's head. Around his neck was a broad collar of sorts, a disk adorned with a ram's horns and entwined golden crocodiles. The little golden crocodiles were alive. They squirmed and entwined and raced around one another.

"Great Lord Sobek, god of the crocodiles of the Nile, called Rager, son of Seth and his consort Neith, nurse of crocodiles, we humbly petition you, as strangers in this land, strangers ignorant of the proper forms, to release this person," Jalil said.

"If you really want to," Christopher muttered under his breath. "Otherwise . . ."

Sobek opened his crocodile mouth, a mouth that could have bit in half any of the crocodiles that could have bit me in half. He said, "She is a witch. She has defiled this river with the touch of her unclean flesh. My children will swallow her flesh and grind her bones."

My fists clenched of their own will. This was impossible. I was trapped, humiliated, and now Jalil was pleading for my life.

"I am sure she is sorry," Jalil said. "I am sure she did not know what she was doing. I am sure that she would do anything to undo the damage she has done. Can you find it in your heart, Lord Sobek, god of the crocodiles of the Nile, called Rager, son of Seth and his consort Neith, nurse of crocodiles, to shower her with your mercy?"

"Release me and I'll —" I began.

The crocodile mouths closed, pressed upper teeth against my flesh, pushed my weight down onto their lower teeth, then stopped, stopped millimeters from piercing my skin with hundreds of teeth.

"Personally I'd shut up and let your lawyer here do the talking," Christopher advised.

I wanted to strangle him. I wanted to rip the insolent tongue from his mouth. I was near swooning from the battle of rage and terror within me. I couldn't reach the glow. Sobek kept it from me, dangled the power just out of my reach.

"We are on our way to see this witch's mother. She is a priestess of Isis," David said, only belatedly adding Sobek's entire title.

"A priestess of Isis?" Sobek repeated thoughtfully.

As he thought that over, the crocodiles' mouths slowly, slowly opened wide. Their upper jaws returned to their more nearly vertical degree.

"Alas, Isis is far away, and she cannot come here, and I cannot go to her," Sobek lamented. "The dam that holds these waters back, the infernal creation of those foul gold-grubbing mortals, blocks my way along the waters."

"The dam?" David wondered.

And at that moment there was a sound of blades slashing at air. A blur of motion, too fast to see. A faint visual impression of brushed copper-colored discs. And seven almost simultaneous impacts, like meat cleavers on a roast.

Coo-Hatch throwing blades.

The upper jaws of the crocodiles fell off, cut neatly, precisely. They simply fell, some forward, toppling onto my shuddering flesh, some splashing into the water. The crocodiles jerked spasmodically, tried to bite, tried to rip me apart, but they were half a pair of pliers.

Reptilian blood stained my legs and arms, drenched my stomach and thighs. I screamed, unable to stop myself, I screamed, expecting death.

But the leering demons were withdrawing, disappointed, fading back into the earth, rushing back to their various masters. And the mutilated crocodiles snapped helplessly, their power gone.

Sobek bellowed an outraged threat. The blades had missed him, had hit only his crocodiles and with unearthly accuracy.

"My children!" the god of crocodiles roared, his own reptilian mouth wide.

David splashed into the water, stabbed his sword downward with all his might into one of the crocodiles blocking his path. He crawled over the doomed creature and grabbed me roughly, yanked me away, toward him, gathered me up, one arm around me and hauled me up the bank, dragging me over mud and rocks to throw me in a wet heap. Then he stood over me, sopping, ragged blue jeans dripping on me, stood over me, sword drawn, ready to kill to protect me.

It had all taken a minute. Maybe less. But every frantic detail of it was burned into my brain, and burned. Burned! I had been rescued. Helpless, I had been saved, by David, by the Coo-Hatch, and by Jalil.

"Here," April said. She had snatched up my clothes and now threw them over me.

"Look what you've done to my crocodiles, my children," Sobek cried in despair. Then, petulantly, "This is none of it proper. None of this has ever been done before, it is all new."

The beasts churned, writhed, lost and confused and doomed now to eventual starvation.

I gathered my clothes, sitting in my own mud patch. Drew shirt and dress over me. Cursed, cursed the world, cursed everything and everyone. I ignored the pain of a dozen deep scratches. Blood seeped from countless small wounds all down my back.

I looked up the riverbank. There atop the rise stood three adult Coo-Hatch accompanied by one flitting juvenile. Their throwing discs had returned to them and now hung from their belts, wiped clean of crocodile blood. They stared at us with royal blue in red eyes.

David gave them a wave. They nodded and withdrew from sight.

Jalil was still playing lawyer with Sobek. But a lawyer with a client now free from immediate threat. "You know what, Sobek? Screw your pet crocodiles. You want some compensation, we can talk. But other than that, we're going to walk."

Sobek's superciliousness was gone now. His crocodile face split into a nasty grin. "I can summon ten times ten crocodiles. I can fill the waters and cover the land with them!"

"Yeah, and our boys back there can slice and dice them," David shot back. "Bring on your crocs, I'm hungry. We'll eat them."

Sobek was taken aback. Alarmed, and more than that, astonished at the notion of being threatened by mere mortals.

"We're going to Egypt," David said. "We're going to see her mother. End of story. You want a fight, we'll arrange that."

"Of course," Jalil added placatingly, "we'd rather get along with you. We're not looking for trouble. Fact is, it would be a lot easier for us if we could go by boat rather than walk the whole way."

Sobek hissed, a reptilian sound. "You cannot pass the dam. The river will not carry you."

"Yeah? Then we'll knock the damn dam down, damn it," Christopher said, obviously convinced he was being funny.

Sobek didn't get the joke. Rather, his malevolent yellow eyes narrowed. "Destroy the dam? Unleash the waters? Do this and Sobek will put aside his terrible wrath."

"Hey, I wasn't volunteering us," Christopher protested.

But I spotted an opening. An opportunity. In the depths of my humiliation, in my lowest moment, I had nevertheless seen the possibilities.

There had always been the question of how we could hope to enter Egypt and survive against all its rigid priesthoods, all its maddening rituals. How to survive in the face of a possibly hostile priestess who was close to Isis. One way: to arrive in Egypt as saviors.

Sobek raised his crocodile eyes to the sky. "Long have I waited here, never hearing from my brothers and sisters in the city. Long years. Years and years, always waiting as I had been bid. This is my place. These are my children. I was exiled for twelve times twelve years for the crime of killing Horus."

His crocodile head lowered sadly. "I was tricked by Seth. And yet the wrath of Isis was great. I was to be kept apart. I would be served by no priests, take part in no rituals. I would receive no sacrifices. Twelve times twelve years I obeyed the sentence. But those years are passed long since and still no summons comes from Isis."

He put his snout down and actually squeezed tears from his murderous eyes.

I stood, pushed my hair back off my face. "We will free the Nile," I announced. "We will free the Nile or you may take us all to feed your children."

"Like hell," Jalil protested.

But Sobek, like most gods, heard what he wanted to hear. We had a deal.

Sobek caused a sailboat to appear, complete with crew. It came gliding up out of nowhere and nosed gently against the shore. It was an odd-looking craft, curved high in front and back. It evoked a cow horn, somehow. The ends were decorated, painted in off-reds and off-greens, forming abstract designs. The whole thing was maybe thirty feet long.

"It's a *dhow,* I guess," David said, frowning at the craft. "Lateen-rigged. Primitive. Look at the rigging. Look at the mast. Or like a cross between a *dhow* and a galley with all those oar ports. Wouldn't last five minutes on the open sea."

The mast was actually three poles leaned together and lashed at the top. A long crossbeam carried a furled sail. There was no wind.

Instead fourteen shirtless, sunburned men

rowed, seven to a side. A fifteenth man stood on a platform at the stern, working a long steering oar.

A swooping, curved shelter made of reeds covered the back third of the boat, providing shade. Within that shade were piled pillows and barrels around a small, low table.

Sobek was gone. He had taken his mutilated crocodiles with him. But the water around the *dhow* was not still. It rippled with barely concealed crocodiles. There might be a hundred of them, just below the surface, out of sight but not out of mind.

The man at the tiller watched us nervously. Presumably he understood that he had been placed at our disposal by the god of crocodiles.

"We're going to lose the Coo-Hatch," David fretted. "No way they'll be able to keep up. I wonder if I should ask them to join us."

"No, so much the better if they stay back," Jalil said.

"What are you talking about, man? They saved our asses twice," Christopher pointed out.

Jalil shook his head. "No, they saved our asses back in Africa. Here they just saved Senna. Look, I'm grateful to them and all, believe me. I was crying back in that tree with the demons and the fire. But look, they're not in control. They could have gotten us killed just now. There's no way the

Coo-Hatch knew for sure that Sobek wouldn't just unload on us. Not saying they didn't try to do right. But they're unpredictable."

"Who isn't unpredictable around here?" April interjected.

"We could have made this same deal with Sobek without slicing and dicing his 'children,'" Jalil pressed. "If you think Gator Head back there is just going to forget all about that — no matter what we do — I think you're crazy. He'll let us knock down this dam, then he'll kill us and enjoy doing it."

"What makes you so sure?" David demanded.

"He's a god of crocodiles. Crocodiles eat their own children. We've messed with a god who has the attributes of a crocodile."

David looked at me for an answer. I stared straight ahead. What was I going to do? Say, "Yes, Jalil is right"?

"Okay, we take the *dhow.* Maybe the Coo-Hatch keep up, maybe not." He led the way aboard and marched straight back to the man at the tiller. The Egyptian stiffened. "How far to this dam?"

"One day's journey, lord. Unless the breeze blows and we are able to raise sail."

"So we get there, what, tomorrow afternoon? Assuming we have to row the whole way?"

The man nodded cautiously.

"Fair enough. You have food on board?"

"Yes, lord. Only poor fare, but good bread, and honey, and dates and cream and wine and —"

"Okay, that's enough. What's your name?"

"Sechnaf, lord."

"Okay, Sechnaf, let's get going. But one thing: Don't bring us into view of the dam during daylight. You understand me? They can't see us coming."

"If they see us, may you cut out my eyes and feed them to the eagles."

David resisted a grin. "Yeah, well, let's just be careful."

I found a place beneath the awning. The pillows were a bit damp and musty but paradise compared to our usual lodgings. The others crowded too near but always keeping a space between me and them.

The boat glided out into the river, leaving the shore behind. I saw an adult Coo-Hatch watching us. He didn't wave, neither did we. Jalil was right, of course; the Coo-Hatch had saved me, but I was glad enough to see them gone. They would never allow any deviation from our mission. They might interfere in ways I could not control.

The food and wine were broken out. David, of course, never drinks alcohol. But the other three did, and they were soon at it, complaining all the while about the muddy flavor.

I drank a glass as well. And I tried to understand how Sobek had cut me off from the power without even exerting himself. What was so special about the gods that they could manipulate the power so much more easily than I?

What were the gods? That was one of the questions I hoped Jalil would answer for me. What were they? A distinct race? Some offshoot of Homo sapiens? Some species of aliens? What exactly were they?

They interbred with humans — did that mean they were humans? That was supposed to be one of the basic definitions of a species, that it can only reproduce with others of its own type.

I was not used to feeling so powerless. And I hated it. I was in the middle, neither human nor god. I had powers but not enough, not enough when some supercilious minor river deity could shut me off from it as easily as a person slamming a door.

I could feel Christopher eyeing me. The wheels were turning in his head, looking for a way to annoy me. He felt he had an advantage over me now. He had seen me naked and helpless and afraid.

"You know, I've heard you can eat alligator

meat," he said. "They say it tastes like chicken. Of course, that's probably just what alligators say about people, huh, Senna?"

I ate a date. Christopher drank his third big cup of wine. Drank it down in a single long swallow.

"You know, I wonder, though," Christopher continued. "I mean, we know you have strange blood, right? I mean, your blood kills plants. Grass. It poisons living things. That's right, isn't it? I mean that was the whole point of that thing back in Africa when Jalil had you all helpless and ready to bleed you out on that tree and kill it."

He lingered over the word *helpless*. Toyed with it.

Despite myself I could not douse the fire that was now lit and burning inside me. The memory of what Jalil had done . . . the fact that twice in just a few days, I had been helpless. Powerless.

I could picture myself carried by Jalil and Thorolf, unconscious, dragged up the tree. I could see myself helpless in the crocodiles' mouths, cut off from the glow, as blind and pathetic as any normal person.

Christopher had seen both of those images, as had April, and, of course, Jalil. David, too, but David I could count on. Mostly.

Christopher swallowed noisily and belched deliberately. "So maybe you would have just killed those poor crocs. Maybe they'd get your blood and curl up and die."

I bent my knees up, wrapped my arms around them, looking like a vulnerable child. But as I did so I put one hand under the hem of my dress and squeezed one of the many scabbed-over tooth marks. Squeezed hard till I felt the sticky wetness.

I smiled at Christopher and moved suddenly. I stood over him and showed him my hand. Blood, my blood, covered two fingers of my hand. I let him stare, let them all stare, uncomprehending, then I plunged both fingers into the wine. I flicked the wine from my fingers and laughed.

"Why not drink it and find out for yourself?" I challenged him.

"That's enough," David snapped.

"Go on, Christopher. Drink," I said. And I did more than speak. I gathered the power to me. I called the power up from the Nile beneath us. No god to stop me now, I drew the power into me, focused it, made myself a lens, sharpened the focus, aimed it at Christopher. Aimed it at his own desire, that was the way. Impossible to force a person to do what he did not want to do. But I could take a desire that already existed and magnify it. That I could do.

"Drink, Christopher," I whispered.

And the cup rose slowly toward his lips. His face was pained, hurt. Like a child who has been punished without cause.

He wanted the wine. He wanted all the wine. He wanted to drink till his mind was reeling, till he staggered and vomited. I could feel it in him, I could feel the drunk in him, the alcoholic just waiting to blossom fully.

And with that desire for the alcohol, a second desire went hand in hand. The desire for me. He and I had been close once. Before I traded him for David. Christopher told himself he didn't care, but he had never gotten over the rejection. He wanted me, some part of me, any part of me. He wanted me to choose him over David.

"Drink," I mouthed silently.

But now I was feeling the weariness, the exhaustion of magic. Using the power drains me. Drawing it into myself that way from the magic river drained me. But I couldn't show that.

Press, Senna, press harder.

All at once Christopher was gulping the wine and David, surprised, jerked toward him, trying to knock it away, but too late.

Christopher, shaking, lowered the cup. He laughed a faint, scared laugh. He was breathing hard. His fingertips were white from the pressure of gripping the cup.

I smiled, magnanimous, as if to say, *See? Nothing to worry about.*

I had to use every last bit of strength to keep from collapsing in a heap. I had pushed too hard. Tried too much. And now my consciousness was swirling, a swoon circled my brain, air all gone, eyes swimming. . . .

No, no, don't pass out. No. Eyes open. Eyes open.

I fought off the exhaustion collapse, kept my feet, kept my face composed. I stumbled on, resuming my seat, but that was nothing, no one would even notice.

No one but Jalil. He watched me with his lizard eyes. He knew what I had done to Christopher and he feared me for it. But he had also seen my weakness, and that fact he added to the other facts stored away in his brain.

Stupid, I realized. I had shown Jalil that I could push Christopher. And I'd shown him that doing it left me drained.

I looked away, refusing to acknowledge his attention. I looked away and felt my eyes blear, lose focus. Tired. I was tired. And my leg hurt where I'd made it bleed.

For some reason I couldn't reach Jalil here. Couldn't touch the exposed nerve of his brain sickness the way I'd just done to Christopher.

Was Jalil protected? No. Absurd. It was a fluke. Some weird fluke. His physical brain here was not a perfect duplicate of his brain in the real world. That had to be it.

Well, maybe I couldn't reach him here, not yet. But there was more than one universe inhabited by Jalil and me. If I couldn't punish one Jalil, I could punish the other.

After a few hours on the river, the others began to fall asleep. I could see their spirits leave them and be sucked back across the universal divide. I felt them go, since, in a way, they traveled through me.

Only David stayed awake, taking the first watch. He was staring into the gathering darkness, trying to figure out what lay ahead. Wondering what he could do. Worrying, always worrying, whether he would be strong enough, quick enough, man enough, enough enough, to win the next battle.

I closed my own eyes, but I did not need sleep to allow me to cross over. My body was entirely within Everworld. I had not split into twinned persons, a real-world Senna and an Everworld Senna, like the others.

But I existed in both places. My soul, to use that clichéd word, my soul lived in both universes. We are all fields, not points. We are expanses, spaces, not locked rooms.

We each extend in many directions, even the dullest human. We are subject and object and all the space between. We are the thing we see, and the thing that sees, and the seer that sees itself, and all the spaces in between.

I extended between universes. I encompassed parts of both. The universes were vast circles that never touched, but I, a much smaller circle, intersected both. A freak of nature. An imperfection. A flaw in what were supposed to be perfect, discrete systems.

I could cross over anytime. It was as easy as letting go. As easy as standing on the parapet of a tall building and simply stepping out into space. But scary, even after so many times. Scary enough that I avoided it.

Scary because the void was no void. Someone, something could see me as I crossed. I felt the mind. Felt its attention. Its interest. It watched me each time. It recognized me.

I never saw it or him or her. I never saw anything as I crossed, there was no light but the glow, and yet I was aware of that presence just the same.

The *dhow,* its deck, its sail now loosed, its crew, all faded from view. The three-dimensional scene around me, with all its subtleties of light and shadow, all its detail, all its sounds, important and not, all of it flattened out, stretched into a piece of transparent film.

I could still see it all, but it seemed to exist only in two dimensions. Flat. Length and breadth but no depth. As if it might disappear entirely if I turned it sideways.

There, beneath the *dhow,* I saw Sobek, crocodile head and human body, swimming with two massive beats as an honor guard. He was following us, watching, waiting.

In the boat, floating above the glowing god, David moved, shifted position, the rowers rowed, the helmsman peed over the side, but all of it was transparent. The water gurgled along the side of the boat, the oars slapped the ripple crests, the planks creaked, a waterbird cried at the setting sun, but all of it was the scratching of a dusty needle on an old vinyl record, a faint recording.

I slid through the two dimensions of it and it wrapped itself around me like a bubble around an intruding finger. Then I was through and falling into darkness, darkness lit only by the awareness of the observer therein.

Far away, a trillion miles, and yet within reach

of my outstretched hand, a different flatness, a different stretched membrane of reality.

It was night there, too. I saw dark faces sleeping. Darkened rooms and ghost-lit streets and prowling cars. Everything connected by wires, everything in place, everything in a box and nothing to spill out.

Everywhere the gasoline ignited, and the gears turned, and the water pushed up into pipes and tanks, and the electricity snapped, and the data streamed, and the waves warped through the air, and nowhere, nowhere the violin-string vibration of enchantment. Nowhere did it glow.

It was so alien to me now. Now that I was away from it, now that I had seen a world where the beautiful glow was everywhere. It was a hungry world where I would never find a meal. It was no longer mine, never had been really. Not my home. Not my people.

I floated above, below, beside the flat membrane of this reality; direction was meaningless. I skimmed like a bird above the surface of some calm, dark, silent lake. I looked for a point to enter, a place I could go, a body that would receive me.

I could project myself, the image of my own body, into this universe, but oh, so exhausting. It meant holding open the doorway between universes, letting the powers of Everworld flow through. And the longer I held that gateway open the more minds would sense my presence. Not the watcher in the void but the smaller minds of Everworld.

When I held open that gate I could feel Loki's eyes searching for me. I knew that Merlin felt the disturbance. I was like someone opening a restaurant door on a freezing night. The warm, comfortable patrons inside all felt the chill, some more, some less, all knowing that a door had been opened.

No, I must not open the door. Easier by far to find an accepting mind. A mind with a weak grip on all that the residents of the real world took for granted.

I could see those minds, those faces, I could sense them, like a bee sensing a flower or a vampire bat sensing warm blood. The mad, they were my prey. The insane, the delusional, the twisted and damaged, they were mine to use.

I saw the one I wanted. His mind twisted and curled around itself, a black hole that distorted the reality before him. A slow whirlpool in reality.

I pushed into the membrane and felt it wrap itself around me, and pushed into the space this creature occupied.

Suddenly I was there. And the world around

me had depth. The world around me had sound. The world around me had smell and taste and texture.

I was back.

"Let's go for a walk," I said, a voice in the head of a madman.

He opened his eyes. He was asleep at the Salvation Army mission. He was three hundred pounds crammed into a narrow army-surplus cot, barely covered by an army-surplus blanket.

"You're not real," he hissed. "Go away now. Don't be bothering me. Go away now, I took my meds."

"You can't get rid of me that easily," I said. It was a voice so small that it would never have moved a sane person. But it would move this lost soul. "I'm with the CIA. You know we can control your brain. You should have worn your tinfoil hat. It's the only way to stop us. Get up, Fat Billy. We have places to go, people to see."

We walked the darkened streets. It wasn't late but the town closed up early. The college kids here were of the serious, studious variety. There were few bars and no clubs.

Serious students and serious citizens. A dull town. A safe town.

Within eight blocks of the lakefront it was all

professionals, the kind of people who commuted south to Chicago every day on Metra or by car or, in more than a few cases, by limo. It was a calm, hardworking, latte-drinking, German/Swedish-sedan-driving community. Lawyers, doctors, investment bankers, stockbrokers, real estate salesmen, businessmen.

Class divisions were all about Lake Michigan. A view of the lake meant you were rich. A view of the lake looking down a cross street meant you were well-off. On the far side of the train tracks you were blue-collar, wanting to cross over to those lake views.

The Salvation Army was, incongruously, just a ten-minute walk from walled, gated, million-dollar mansions. It shared a block with the half-way house for the mentally ill. Fat Billy had lived in both places. He survived by waylaying businessmen and women and stroller ladies on their way through the park to the train station. He had a strangely sweet voice and looked like a gigantic baby. He would ask for spare change and praise God if he got some. And then he would walk along, muttering about the CIA, the aliens, the government always trying to control him.

I grew up in this town after my mother deposited me in the lap of my father and his loving family. We didn't front the lake, but we were close enough to catch a slight view past another house.

I had hated the house from the start. And learned to hate the town as well. The rich were dull snobs. The near-rich were just as dull and even bigger snobs. The working-class kids suffered from a dual inferiority complex: They were neither lakefront nor hard-core Chicago.

Why had she left me there? Why, when she knew what I was? She had traveled the world — was there no other, better place for me? Was there no place where I could have grown up with at least a chance of finding a life for myself?

It was the very heart and soul of prosperous, early-twenty-first-century America. Not a time or place for a witch. In earlier days I might have been drowned or hanged or burned, but I'd have been less bored.

Fat Billy walked the streets making a sort of soft keening sound. He was cold. It was a windy fall night and his coat didn't close in front.

We passed one of the ridiculously numerous churches that are the chief architectural feature of the town. In the historic district there's a massive, ugly church on every corner.

I looked up at the high bell tower, a gray shadow against an overcast night sky. The family church. I had spent some of my most enjoyable hours there. The enforced quiet, the ritual, the expectation of magic had always appealed to me. I loved the liturgy, the call and response, the kneeling and standing, the singing.

I would sit there and lose myself in the rite, release my own distracting thoughts, and in that meditation I would find the strange power within myself. It was there that I became fully aware of my potential.

It was a toy at first, a trick that I could do that no one else knew about. I could sit there and cause a man in the row ahead of me to scratch his ear, or a woman to adjust her hair. Minor mind tricks. Easier because the people were in the same meditative state as I was.

I knew instinctively to keep this to myself. I knew I was different. I knew that my own mother had feared me and that sad truth made me strong.

But I was ignorant, too. Nowhere to turn for understanding, no one to ask for an explanation of what I was, why I was different. What was I going to do? Go to my stepmother? My guidance counselor? My priest?

Father, I feel a strange power inside of me. It feels as if the fabric of the world is somehow turned inside out. Like there's a hole in my mind, and not an empti-

ness, Father, but a fullness. A door opens and I see a swirling light show of forms and shapes and colors. Three dimensions become four and six and twelve. And when I focus my mind, when I release my mind and empty it of all thoughts and at the same time bring it into razor-sharpness, Father, I can draw those forms and colors up inside myself and push with it, prod with it, reach with it like it's another hand, an invisible hand whose fingers can touch minds.

I could have asked for help. But I didn't want help making it stop. I wanted help making it grow. I wanted to know how far I could take it. Wanted to know how to build my stamina, resist the crippling weariness.

If I had asked those and all my other questions, I would have ended up like Fat Billy. No burning the "different," not in this place, in this time. No torch-and-pitchfork mob crying, "Burn the witch!" Just a man in a white coat with a handful of pills. The power of technology. The dark magic of science.

The only other interesting part of the town for me, from the age of seven onward, was that psychiatric halfway house where the crazy folks sat outside in the grim little courtyard and chain-smoked and let their medications do battle with their voices. I never felt I was one of them. But I wondered sometimes whether they at least glimpsed what I alone seemed able to see clearly.

I liked the crazies. I had liked Jalil for his craziness.

But that former affection wouldn't stop me from hurting him now.

I stood on the street in the darkness outside Jalil's house. Whoever, whatever kept him safe from me in Everworld would not protect him here.

Chapter VII

After a while I slipped back across the barrier and became fully present in Everworld once again. David was asleep now and Jalil had taken over the watch. He was in the bow, up by the sheltered candle that was our only light.

The sail had been raised. A breeze was blowing us along and most of the rowers lay asleep on their benches.

I wanted to taunt Jalil. I wanted to ask him whether he'd had a good time over in the real world. Wanted to ask him whether seven hand washings had been enough, or had it perhaps required seven times seven to silence the mad voice in his head.

But that wouldn't be smart.

Fat Billy had stood out on Jalil's lawn and screamed till the police came to take him away.

He had screamed that the CIA was telling him to cut off his own filthy hands. He screamed it again and again. The CIA wanted him to cut off his hands, they were so dirty, he didn't want to, don't make me, but the voices kept saying it.

I knew Jalil had heard. I saw him in his bedroom window. I saw the frightened, haunted look in his eyes. Oh, Jalil, you saw a mirror of yourself there, didn't you? You saw your own weakness magnified into shrieking insanity.

Oh, and it bothered you, didn't it, Jalil? And now you aren't seeing me in your mind at all, are you, Jalil? Not seeing images of Senna helpless and weak in the mouths of crocodiles. Not savoring the rush of triumph you felt as you hauled me unconscious into that tree. No, Jalil, your mind is full of that screaming voice, full to overflowing with bitter memories of your own helpless reaction.

You scrubbed till the blood came, didn't you, Jalil? Scrubbed and wept and saw yourself for the pitiful, twisted weakling you are.

I felt a physical pleasure, an intense rush of shuddering sensation, a wave of anger released and hurt avenged. I closed my eyes and let it pass through me, let it linger. The power, I loved it so, it filled me and fulfilled me.

I could handle Jalil. I could handle them all.

David's insecurity, Christopher's addictions, April's hatred, they all made me strong.

And yet I could not defeat even a minor Egyptian deity. That darkened my mood. I had escaped Loki, but Hel had defeated me easily, and I had known that Athena could do the same. Now this measly god of crocodiles who still followed us, watched us, waited . . . For what?

How would I find the might to resist them? I would never be Loki's gateway. I would never be Ka Anor's slave. But how long could I get by on manipulation, deceit, and a handful of minor tricks? How long till my own secret, unsuspected force, my hidden allies, could be brought to bear?

I still needed Jalil. That fact burned, but it was a fact. Jalil wanted to break into the software of Everworld. "Software" was his word, his limited concept, but it was accurate enough, probably. The great high gods, Odin and Zeus and the Daghdha and Quetzalcoatl and Amon-Ra and the other father gods, the great powers, had created Everworld. They had written its laws and encoded them in magic.

Jalil called it software. To me it was spells and incantations. But there was no real difference there. David, Christopher, April, none of them cared to pry up the floorboards and find out what was underneath, but Jalil did. Of course he did: He wanted to understand and control himself.

David stirred, woke, disturbing my reverie.

He joined Jalil and spoke in a whisper, but a whisper that carried clearly over the soft, lullaby sounds of the water and the boat.

"We're making good time." David yawned. "We been moving like this for long?"

"Since I took over for Christopher," Jalil confirmed. "He said the wind came up about an hour before he went off."

"No way the Coo-Hatch could keep up. Hope they don't think we stiffed them somehow."

"No. I think we were even. You . . . prepaid . . . for that second save, for them saving Senna. You gave them the rifling idea. Hell, they owe us."

David looked back, suddenly aware that they might be overheard. "I better go talk to what's his name. The guy."

"Sechnaf," Jalil supplied.

"Yeah." David walked past me, joined the helmsman. "Sechnaf, how are we doing on time? We look to be making a good nine or ten knots."

"I don't understand, lord," the Egyptian replied, baffled by the concept of knots. "We move swiftly. We will arrive at the dam before the sun rises. If my lord commands, we could hide in the mouth of a tributary, concealed in the reeds, till night comes again."

David considered that. "If we wait, we risk being found out. On the other hand, we can't attack when we don't even know what's what. How far from this hiding place to the actual dam?"

"Half a morning's rowing, in still waters."

David sighed. "Which means squat to me except it isn't too far. Thanks, Sechnaf. Take her into that tributary. Hey —" He snapped his fingers. "Any way we can snag one or two of the smaller boats I've seen around? Little rowboat deals, look like they're made out of bamboo?"

"You have but to command, lord."

"Fine. Do it. I want at least one small boat. I want it lightly provisioned with water and bread."

He came and squatted down by me. I looked at him, curious. "I'm taking Jalil and going in to scout this dam," he said. "You're coming, too."

"Me?" I was surprised.

"I can't take everyone, and I can't leave you behind with Christopher and April. You're becoming a bigger and bigger pain in the ass, Senna. I can't trust you not to push April's buttons or start Christopher drinking. Besides, that whole shape-changing illusion you do could be helpful."

"I'm not one of your soldiers, David."

"Yeah? Well, you're the one who promised Gator Head we would knock down this dam of his. You figure you get to just set the agenda, then sit back and watch us do the work?"

There was little I could say to that. "I'll be happy to come along."

"Fine. Good. You and I will need to get some of the grease they use to lubricate the oarlocks. That'll take the shine off our white skin. Go ahead. I'll talk to Jalil."

It was another hour before the *dhow* glided into the reed-choked mouth of a small stream. Everyone was up by then and my face was smeared with grease. Christopher was itching to make a crude joke, but his better angels were in charge, for the moment.

"Okay, here's the deal," David explained. "The three of us are going over the side. We'll row the rowboat downstream, try and catch a look at what's up. Then we'll pull our way back here. April? Christopher? This *dhow* does not leave here till we get back, you got that? Sechnaf tries to leave, you convince him otherwise. Convince him however you have to." He made a gesture that Christopher and April would understand and no one else in Everworld would: He pointed his index finger at his temple and cocked his thumb.

Christopher laughed. "Dude, if we had some of those, this whole universe would be working for us."

David leaped, surefooted, down into the rocking, unsteady little boat. He and Jalil handed me down. Then Jalil came down, gawky, awkward, saved by David from falling overboard.

David took the oars. Jalil offered, but David knew what he was doing and Jalil did not. Besides, David likes hard physical work.

We separated from the ship and instantly the current caught us up. Night swallowed the *dhow* and April and Christopher, and we were alone. Or so it seemed.

David rowed. I sat silent. I let myself slip between universes, just enough to disengage, just enough to sense whether Sobek was still there. The crocodile god watched, eyes above the murky water.

David, voice low, said, "Jalil, man, what do you know about dams?"

"What do I know about dams? What? I know nothing about dams."

David grunted, worked the oars to keep us in the swiftest part of the current. "Me neither. I guess we'll learn."

There were no lights on the riverbanks, just the shadows of swaying palm trees that blacked out irregular patches of the amazing array of stars. The moon was not yet risen and none of us could see beyond the boundaries of the boat. Barely that much. But I had the sense that we were moving fast. The breeze that blew on our backs was stilled by our own matching speed.

"Shhh," David said and lifted up his oars.

I strained to hear. Yes, sounds. Unguarded sounds. Singing. Deep, harsh voices. A rough choir composed entirely of bass and baritone.

David steered out of the strongest current and we drifted along, silent, holding our breath.

Then, coming suddenly into view, a row of flickering torches, searingly bright to eyes straining to see by starlight. The torches seemed to float above the river, a cordon stretched across. I blinked and stared hard and could see the outlines of the dam: massive timbers and crossbeams. And then, manlike shapes moving between pools of torchlight.

David mouthed, "I'm going to beach her. No sound."

We drifted a bit more and suddenly the tangle of a bush reached down and caught my hair. I stifled my impulse to yell. More bushes, I ducked down, and the boat slid to a stop.

David was out in an instant, barely making a splash. He pulled the boat up onto what might have been a small, shallow beach. Impossible to say. The darkness was almost complete. The darkness of a world before electricity.

We had lost direct sight of the dam but could still see the glow of the torches through the trees.

"Come on," David said almost soundlessly. "Stay close. Stay low. Don't trip. If you do trip don't make a damned sound."

I was behind David, Jalil behind me. We stayed within arm's length of one another; it would be too easy to get separated and lost. How would we ever find our way back to the boat?

The dam had seemed so close but it took half an hour of wading through tepid water, slopping through wet sand, and fighting the weeds that slapped at us as we passed till we could see the dam clearly again. I was filthy and wet and worn out. My legs and arms and face had been whipped by unseen branches, unseen obstacles. My palms were skinned from falling.

There was a house. An ordinary house with stone walls and a flat roof. Someone's farmhouse, once upon a time before the dam was built. The water was up to midwindow. A man, a fish, or a crocodile could swim easily in and out of the windows.

From the roof I could see most of the dam. I could see it too well; we were too close. The dam was tall. It rose ten feet or more above the water's level on the upstream side. There was no way to see the downstream side, to guess how much lower the river was once it resumed its course.

There were strong stone blockhouses guarding the two ends of the dam, one quite near to us and higher up. If the moon came out we'd be easily visible. I could probably throw a rock through that window from where I stood. The singing we'd heard came from that nearby blockhouse. The voices sang about a great warrior who slew a dragon and took his gold.

I wondered if any of that was true. I had seen dragons. They were hard to rob and harder to kill.

Guards patrolled the dam, stumping along a narrow walkway. I couldn't see faces or details but there was no missing the fact that they were shorter than men, also broader. They looked as if they'd been carved out of perfect cubes, almost as wide as they were tall. Axes glinted in their hands. Torchlight set off the dull shine of chain-mail shirts.

David looked a question at me. But Jalil answered before I could.

"Dwarfs," he whispered. "Remember Hel's harem city?"

David looked puzzled. He was not the only one. What were dwarfs doing here? This was the sacred Nile. This was Egypt. Dwarfs were a European myth. And how had dwarfs been able to defend a dam in defiance of the gods of Egypt?

David watched a while longer, taking mental notes. At last he nodded. "Okay."

We began to climb down. I slipped, a chunk of water-rotted adobe flew out from under my foot, clattered and splashed.

David grabbed me, lifted me, and slid down into the water. Jalil was right behind us. A hard voice cried, "Who goes? Friend or foe, declare yourself!"

Then, "Foes at the gate! Foes at the gate!"

Torches were being lit, twice, three times as many as before. Dwarfs ran from the blockhouse out onto the dam. But others emerged from the landward side. Four of them raced around toward our position. I heard the clatter of weapons.

We were up to our waists in water, no way to outrun them. Not without making noise, not without being seen. And now, with exquisite bad timing, a low, crescent moon began to emerge from behind a cloud.

David held me close, pressed his mouth to my ear, and said, "If you have some trick, now's the time."

Then he snatched Jalil's shirt and yanked him down. The two of them squatted in the water, only their heads above the surface. I heard them drawing shaky breaths, getting ready. I knew that under the water David was drawing his sword.

The dwarfs clumped toward us, loud, grumbling, threatening, kicking, and cursing their way through bushes and reeds.

I breathed deeply myself, and with the exhalation I released the conscious part of me, the questing, rational mind. I let my thoughts drift away and opened myself up to the power.

Then, all at once, there they were, four thick, dangerous-looking creatures with bristling beards, axes at the ready. David and Jalil submerged, disappeared.

The dwarfs stared, dumbstruck, motionless, axes held loose, forgotten.

"The Lady," one whispered, his rough voice reverential.

"The Lady! How may we serve you?"

"Yes, the Lady," a third said, skeptical. "Unless it is wizardry."

I couldn't let skepticism take hold. "It is I, your Lady. Tell me what you wish, honorable dwarfs. Why have you built this magnificent dam?"

They liked that. They puffed with pride.

"There is gold to be had, Lady. The river carries gold dust in the sediment. We draw off the water into sluices and can extract gold."

"That must be harsh labor, dwarfs, so far from your homes," I said, very concerned. "I mourn to see my . . ." My what? I was making this up. My what? What should I call them? "I mourn to see my faithful servants labor so far from home."

"Aye," one agreed. "But the gold will be where it will, Lady, and we must follow the vein where it leads."

They all nodded sagely.

"Tomorrow, at first light, I will show you a vein of gold richer than any seen since the days of your fathers. A place where nuggets as big as your fists lie on the surface, just waiting to be picked up! You will fill wagons full of it!"

They liked that. Four bearded faces lit up. They were gnarled, weather-beaten, scarred, hard faces, but they had become the faces of children sitting on Santa's lap.

"Gold?" one whispered, as though the word itself might be magic. He looked at his fist to get an idea of the nuggets I promised.

"In return you will build a shrine to me, there, where you now stand!"

"How . . . how large a shrine? How expensive?"

Greedy and *cheap,* I thought. But fortunately credulous as well. Cynicism is rare in Everworld. Doubt is unusual in a place where the gods not only exist, but can be seen on a regular basis.

"Go!" I ordered and pointed back to the dam. "Go and prepare yourselves to become rich beyond your wildest imaginations! Go now! But do not forget my shrine, lest you lose all you gain."

They went. They looked back over their shoulders, but they went, walking faster and faster, bunching up, slapping one another on the back. They were scared, nervous, unsure, but the vision of gold was too strong to be ignored.

David and Jalil rose, struggled to draw breath without gasping. We retreated quickly, silently. It would never do for "the Lady" to be heard splashing around. Nor would it do for some brighter, more inquisitive dwarf to come back looking for the golden vision of the Lady, only to find me dripping like a wet dog.

Half an hour later we were back on the river with David rowing hard against the current, hugging the still waters by the far shore.

"What did you do?" Jalil asked me.

"A little magic," I said. "I know how you love magic, Jalil."

"But what? What did they see?"

I shrugged. I was cold. Tired. "They saw a shining, beautiful woman with gold earrings and gold necklaces and a golden band around her waist."

"You're that familiar with dwarf mythology?"

I laughed. "Every mythology has some figure of a beautiful lady who rises from the waters. Sometimes more than one. It was a safe bet that the dwarfs had one as well. I assumed theirs would involve gold."

David said, "You just bluffed them? You were just guessing?"

"A little better than a guess," I said. "People are fairly predictable, you know. Their gods are strong, wise men and evil, deceitful men and beautiful, virginal women. Mostly. Not always, but mostly. There are variations."

"Yeah, well, you saved our asses," David said.

I waited for Jalil's thanks, but it wasn't forthcoming.

Instead he asked David, "So, did you figure out some brilliant way to knock that dam down?"

"Yeah."

"Really?"

"I think so. As long as old Gator Head doesn't mind not getting his *dhow* back."

The sun was blistering hot by the time we made it back to the *dhow.* David and Jalil had taken turns at the oars, and we'd had to pull over to the shore on several occasions, tie the boat off, and let them rest.

April was on anxious lookout when we at last came around the bend and into the mouth of the tributary.

We climbed aboard and David announced, "I'm sleeping for a few hours, then I'll talk. In the meantime, Sechnaf, I want you to beach us over there and get your crew to start gathering up all the dry reeds, grass, palm fronds, anything dry that will burn. Fill this boat. Just leave room for the men to work their oars."

"What are we doing, Admiral?" Christopher demanded.

"Something I read about in Patrick O'Brian. It's called a fire ship." He held up a hand, forestalling more inquiries. "No more questions, I'm beat."

With that, he flopped down in a shady corner on some pillows and was snoring within minutes. I felt him pass through me on the way back to the real world.

"Fire ship?" Christopher repeated. "I'm guessing that's pretty much self-explanatory. I'll just go wait over on shore."

I found Sechnaf giving orders to his men. He accepted David's authority. Perhaps he had direct instructions from Sobek. But it was also true that David had acquired the habit of issuing orders and expecting to be obeyed. It was a sort of natural magic. The more you gave orders and were obeyed, the more easily you gave orders. Men are sheep and love to be led.

I had chosen well with David. In fact, he had done better than I'd hoped. And even if he was no longer entirely under my control, he still ended up doing my bidding. I was content with that.

Still, the time would come when I would have to take him down several notches. A pawn that crosses the entire board can become a queen. Not perhaps the title David would appreciate, but the principle was clear: There was one ruler in this group and it was me.

I sat on pillows and drank a bowl of watered-down mead. I had come to like the drink. It was fermented honey, too sweet, too strong, but with enough water it became harmless enough.

I let my mind wander, ignoring the coming and going of the Egyptians as they handed armloads of grass and fronds and branches up into the boat. They chanted as they worked, a repetitive, meditative chant praising various gods.

What would it be like, seeing my mother again? What should I say? What would she say? What play would she make? What scene should we act out? The prodigal daughter? The vengeful spawn?

One thing was sure: I would have to be very careful. She was strong or she would not be in Everworld. She had crossed over, that night in my father's office. She had warped reality, opened a gateway to Everworld, and left nothing behind but me and my pale and quaking father.

Worse yet, she was a priestess of Isis. I had learned about Isis. I'd read all I could find about Isis. She was called "great in magic." Like all Egyptian deities, her role had changed over time, as society needed. She was a mother god, a sorceress, the wife of her brother, Osiris.

Osiris had been killed by Seth, a god of chaos, a sort of Egyptian Loki. Despite being dead, Osiris had gone to rule the Underworld and had still managed, by virtue of Isis' great magic, to impregnate her. She had a son by her dead brother/husband. The son was named Horus. He was a god of the sky, of birds of prey.

Or had been. If Sobek was telling the truth, Horus was dead now, too. And Isis had raged against Sobek for more than a century.

None of which told me exactly what I would be facing when at last I found my mother. The Egyptian gods were not the Greeks. The Greeks wrote stories with a Western sensibility. They could be odd, but the Greek myths could be understood in linear fashion, A to B to C. The Egyptians were less direct. Each god had a dozen faces, a dozen forms, a dozen attributes, often weirdly mismatched. Or at least that was the story deciphered from a millennium's worth of hieroglyphics.

The truth? We would soon see.

I was excited by the possibilities. Anxious, too. Maybe afraid.

A part of me, too large a part of me, wanted to go to that old witch and cry, "Mommy, why? Why did you leave me? Why did you leave me in a world where I could never hope to fit in? Why did you leave me with a father who feared me and a stepmother who despised what I represented and a sister whose hatred would burn bright for all the years of my childhood? Why?"

Well, I wouldn't do that. I wouldn't give her that satisfaction.

I had survived. I had escaped the real world, with a bit of inadvertent help from Loki and his son Fenrir. And now, Mom, now your little girl is on her way to becoming a power all on her own.

Yes, little Senda is a pathway, all right. Her own pathway.

I closed my eyes and savored the possibilities. I saw myself in my own temple, atop a mountain, up in the clear air, up in the clouds.

I saw the gods of the Greeks, so reduced that they could only lend their power to me for my own uses. I saw the monster Ka Anor exterminated, his awful hive laid waste. I saw Merlin trapped in a prison from which there was no escape, stewing in his own impotence, begging for an audience with me. And Loki? Loki would serve me, a useful tool.

I would hold all the reins of real power, play one god against the next, balance them, trick them, use them as they used mere mortals.

They saw me as a witch. A gateway. A mutant freak who lived in both universes at once. To the gods I was a tool or an impediment. But they did not fear me, oh not yet. They didn't fear me because they didn't understand. They didn't see the crucial fact.

Of course the gods didn't get it, how could they? When they had left the old world, humans had carried swords and sharpened sticks. How could they guess how far behind they had fallen?

But Jalil could have figured it out, would have, if only he had opened his mind. April had a CD player in her backpack. The batteries still worked. The tiny laser still read the invisible coded bumps on the CD and music still issued forth.

If a CD player . . .

Haven't thought of that yet, have you, Jalil? Haven't figured it out, have you, smart, smart boy? You think I want to bring all the monsters of Everworld into the real world? For what purpose, you smug fool? What would I gain?

Ah, clever, clever Jalil, you've missed the crucial fact: A gate swings open in both directions.

I laughed happily to myself. Oh yes, it was all there for me. I simply had to stay alive long enough to prepare the groundwork.

Then, for Jalil. Then, for my mother. Then, for my sister. Then all of them. All of them.

As night fell the oarsmen rowed the *dhow* out into the channel. David explained what was needed.

"It's a wooden dam and they've coated it with some kind of tar to keep the wood from rotting. I noticed that their lights, their torches, are all cantilevered out over the water. That means the dwarfs are worried about fire. Which is good for us."

"But it can only burn down to the water line," Jalil pointed out.

"I'm hoping that's all we'll need," David said. "My guess is, hope is anyway, is that the structure will be so weakened it will collapse."

April said, "Won't that cause some huge flood when all the water is released?"

David nodded. "Yeah."

April laughed incredulously. "And so we're just going to do it anyway? People could get killed."

David glanced at me, as though blaming me or at least hoping I would offer a justification.

It was Christopher who said, "Look, we do this or we end up neck-deep in crocodiles. We promised Gator Head. Besides, these dwarfs are foreigners, right? They came here, put up this dam, the Egyptians weren't for it, obviously."

David tried to move back to practical considerations. "We need to steer the ship toward the spillway. The current should do that for us, but —"

"No. Stop," April demanded. "Hey, the whole reason we're on this trip to Egypt is because we gave the Coo-Hatch the knowledge to make gunpowder. Haven't we learned a lesson here about just running around carelessly messing with things?"

It was my turn. "Egypt relies on the Nile and its floods to fertilize the land. This dam keeps the floods from happening. It is very likely that people downstream are starving as a result. We're saving Egypt, not hurting her."

"You don't know that. You can't know that, Senna," she snapped. "This was all your idea, anyway, wasn't it? So once again, here we go following Senna's orders, doing her dirty work. Don't you guys see that?"

"The dwarfs are robbing the Egyptians of their gold and starving them in the process," I said flatly. "We're on the side of the angels here."

April sneered. "Anytime you're on the side of the angels, the angels need to change sides."

But she made no further objections. She'd earned her little gold star for the day. And she was no more interested in becoming crocodile food than I was.

We climbed down the sides of the *dhow* into the rowboats. Three small boats, with just enough room for the crew as well.

David stayed aboard and took the steering oar from Sechnaf. A small fire burned in a ventilated clay pot. The dry grass was piled high. The mast and sail had been splashed with flammable oil.

"You are going to get off, right?" Jalil called up to David.

"No, I'm going to go down with the ship," David said with rare sarcasm.

"He would, you know," Christopher muttered.

Down the river we glided, slow as the current. No one rowed, only steered. We were a weird, stately parade, retracing the path we had taken earlier. Silent but for the sounds of wood and water.

Then we rounded a bend and saw the line of torches. Closer we drifted. No signal from David. And closer. Close enough to see dim shadowy shapes in the torchlight. And slowly, slowly closer still.

A cry in the night.

"A boat! Alarm, alarm, a boat! Foes at the gate! Foes at the gate!"

More torches now, and the sound of scabbards clattering against chain-mailed thighs.

The dwarfs were rushing from both blockhouses, out onto the dam. They formed into a line of battle, clearly expecting an attack. Ax blades glinted. I could almost see faces.

David wrapped a rope around the oar, lashing it into place. Then he kicked the clay pot. It twirled, throwing off fireworks, drops of burning oil that landed on straw and fronds and branches and reeds.

The fire did not erupt all at once. At first it was just a few flickers here and there, not even directly visible to us down below in the boats.

Then a gust of wind and all at once, like a living thing, like a match head, the fire erupted, leaped up, roared, caught the wind. It swirled up around the mast, throwing showers of sparks everywhere.

David dove into the water. The dwarfs cried out, dismayed, realizing now that they were helpless, that their weapons were irrelevant.

The *dhow,* a blindingly bright, impossibly huge

bonfire, drifted steadily, inexorably toward the dam.

Dwarfs hesitated, stood firm, then all broke at once. They raced back toward shore as the flaming heap slammed, crunched, rolled against the dam, pressed against the spillway by the force of the current.

The banks of the river, the blockhouses, the trees, all were painted orange and yellow. Dwarfs ran, in and out of flickering shadows, ran, scattering into the woods. The dam itself was burning now. The flames raced left along the dam, fanned by the breeze.

The fire cracked and popped and roared, sucking the wind into its vacuum. The ragged crest of the flames soared a hundred feet high. I felt the heat on my face, my cheeks burned, I wondered if my hair would catch fire. It was like standing near a star, an inferno surrounded by blackness.

Sechnaf and one crewman and Christopher were in the rowboat with me. David appeared, wet, spitting muddy water. He pulled himself up into the boat with a little help from Christopher.

He squeegeed water out of his hair and watched his handiwork. "That will burn for a while," he remarked. "We better pull into shore. Everyone stay on alert. If we run into any dwarfs they aren't going to be happy with us."

Our three little boats turned and began to pull back against the current, away from the inferno we had created. We landed on a muddy bank by a small stand of dying palms.

The dam was out of direct sight but the glow of the flames lit up the night.

"Hell of a bonfire," Christopher said. "Now what, General Sherman?"

Jalil looked sharply at him. Jalil's last name is Sherman.

"General Sherman, dude," Christopher clarified. "The guy who burned Atlanta? Didn't you ever see *Gone With the Wind*?"

"Now we wait and see what happens," David said. "No one sleeps. Everyone keep your weapons handy. Watch the woods."

And the water, I thought. But I said nothing. We had done as Sobek wanted. But that didn't mean he would refrain from killing us.

Perhaps not tonight. No, surely not tonight, not, at least, till he was sure we'd succeeded.

As David stood watch, I let myself drift back across the void. Back to the real world.

David was not the only general. I had my own troops to lead.

It was exhausting work. I had to project my own physical self, or at least an illusion of myself, back into the real world. And in this case not some familiar picture of my true self — I needed a modified image, one I had invented some weeks earlier for just this purpose.

It required extreme effort. And even more effort to create the wonders and miracles that my troops demanded.

They met in a small room in the back of a dirty-windowed T-shirt store down in Rogers Park. The neighborhood was at the northern extreme of Chicago. A mix of nationalities and religions, immigrants of all types. A working-class neighborhood of brick apartment buildings with rusty window-unit air conditioners and small frame houses with carefully kept yards. The avenues were lit by the neon of check-cashing storefronts, doughnut shops, and twenty-four-hour gas stations.

The room itself was four bare walls, a single eye-level window blocked with black construction paper, stained carpet, and six rows of folding chairs.

My troops had built a sort of altar for me. A pitiful six-inch-high platform painted black and surmounted by a large crate disguised by a drapery of red felt.

On the bare white wall behind this altar was a poster. It showed two ellipses, separated, but joined together by a muscular male figure holding an ellipse in each hand. All this was rendered in gold on a dark green background.

The male figure was me. Of course, not precisely me. My own natural form didn't fit the image required. I needed men to follow me, I needed killers, I needed the proper mix of credulous sheep and determined psychopaths. And for those people I needed a male god, not a female.

I floated above the room, unseen, unseeable, above the two-dimensional picture of the room, projected translucent on the bubble-skin of the real world. I saw into their minds, into their darkness, their emptiness.

Eighteen of them. Four more than last time.

Good. I skimmed above the new ones, slid within millimeters of their minds, touched the electrical field that snapped the synapses of their gray-pink brains.

Sheep. All of them were mere sheep. That was fine. I needed sheep. Sheep made fine servants, and they were no danger to me.

Besides, I had others. I slid above the universe and found the mind that glowed red in my imagination. I felt it, felt the twisted rage there. I felt the resentment, the failure, the absence of hope, the void.

A dangerous one here. A true psychopath. He had come twice before, and he was back for a third time. He was young but so much the better; he would be wilder and yet more easily controlled.

Do you believe in me yet, Keith? I wondered. Have you accepted me as the only path to fulfillment? Have you abandoned those other fools with their ridiculous ideologies? Are you ready to accept the fact that magic, only magic, can save you from the life you are now destined to live?

I drew all my powers about me. I drained power from Everworld, carried it across the blank void, called up a hundred times more than I should need, because so much was lost in transit.

I was tired already and yet could not show it. I

formed the image of the god I had invented: hard-faced, stern, steel-gray hair cut military short. I showed only my head and shoulders, and my shoulders were draped in folds of blazing white. I was a god, a general, a father, a leader, a brilliant madman, because of course they needed a madman.

I focused all my power and slid into the real world. A gasp from every mouth. All eyes stared. Pulses accelerated.

I shone upon their upturned faces; they couldn't believe it, couldn't and yet could. Would.

Keith turned, as he always did, looking for the trick, trying to spot some projector. He wanted so much to believe, needed to, but I was asking him to change loyalties and that was hard.

I spoke in a harsh, commanding tone. "You have come as ordered." I allowed a slight nod, no more, no gratitude, because they were required to be here, they had been ordered to be here.

"We are assembled and await your orders, Great One." The reedy sycophantic voice of a man named Dawkins. He was my high priest.

"Report," I snapped.

He stiffened, an amateur trying to approximate a professional military stance. "Yes, Great One. Your holy arsenal has been increased by twelve fully automatic weapons, two cases of hand grenades, and —" He paused for effect and swelled with pride. "Four grenade launchers."

I nodded. "Well done, men. Well done. And I see four new warriors here. But we need still more. Only when we have a hundred well-armed men, all sworn to our cause, can we move to the next level and begin the mighty work that lies before us."

"What . . . ?" One of the new people had blurted without thinking. He looked abashed, worried by his own temerity.

"You want to know what this mighty work is?" I said, gritting illusory teeth, then grinning a hard smile. "I will show you, men, I will show you."

I paused, gathering my energy like a weightlifter readying himself to heft some impossible weight.

I opened the gate, just a crack, just a bit, but what these creatures felt and heard and saw was a blast, an assault of imagery that bypassed their eyes and ears and erupted full-dimensional in their minds.

They saw Loki's castle and Huitzilopoctli's sparkling city and Nidhoggr atop his mountain of gold. They saw Fenrir and the Midgard Serpent and Galahad in his armor. They saw Olympus itself and all its gods. They saw Ka Anor and his

Hetwan hordes. And they saw gold and palaces and castles and thrones.

They gasped. They cried out. They felt the realness of it, they knew it was all true, too intense to be anything but real.

And as they gaped, entranced, swelling with greed and power lust, I said, "All of it will be ours! All of it will belong to us! We will march with the might of our world to invade and subdue another world. Each of you a king! And I as your god!"

"What do you command, Great One?" Dawkins practically sobbed.

"The time has come. You must make careful plans. But you must bring more weapons. Weapons of great power to batter down the walls of proud castles!"

Dawkins frowned. "Great One, do you mean artillery? Mortars?"

Did I mean artillery? I was weak on the terminology. I should have learned more. Should have researched. I could still screw up the illusion by seeming less than omniscient.

But Keith rescued me without knowing it. He was anxious to put himself forward. Anxious for my love, you see.

"The National Guard armory," he said. "They have mortars and shells and all. And I know a guy . . ."

"Then make it so!" I commanded, wobbly with exhaustion. "Make it so, before I come again!"

I disappeared, collapsed, fell in on myself, sank, floating, barely conscious, back into Everworld. Back into the frail body that knelt in the dark by the bank of the Nile.

I moaned softly and fell facedown in the dirt. I lay there, not caring if the others saw. I was empty. Not a spark of energy left in me. Immobile.

As if from far off I heard a sustained crash, a roar, and saw the inferno's light dim.

"There goes the dam," David commented.

I smiled, content. We would enter Egypt as heroes. And over in the real world my little army was growing.

Jalil looked down at me, not exactly sympathetic, but curious.

"You all right?" he asked.

"I'm fine," I managed to whisper.

Fine, Jalil. We will enter Egypt as heroes. And my army grows. Before too much longer, Jalil, you'll see how foolish you were.

The gate opens both ways, you see.

Let the monsters of Everworld into the real world? Of course not. What would that gain me?

But let the monsters of the real world come here and bring their tools of destruction? The CD player had crossed the divide and continued to work. If a CD player, why not a gun? And as David the general had said, a contest of guns versus swords was over quickly.

What should I call myself when my rule was complete? Queen? Goddess?

Time enough to worry about all of that.

In the morning we left Sechnaf's men behind to find their way home. We discovered the boats resting high and dry. The river had dropped precipitously and we had to drag the rowboats across a hundred yards of sucking mud to reach the river.

The river was content. The river was no longer frustrated, I could feel it. The river was carrying out its charge, flowing as it should from source to sea.

"Shouldn't Gator Head give us an escort?" Christopher demanded. "I mean, we cleared the river, right?"

"I don't think gods are good at gratitude," Jalil said. "Let's just be happy he didn't try to kill us out of sheer spite."

We used only two of the boats. Christopher

and April in one; David, Jalil, and I in the other. Our boat took the lead, but we stayed close, sometimes side by side.

We soon reached the wreckage of the dam. It had collapsed in the middle, a wide, jagged hole through which the river swelled and rushed and churned triumphantly. The dam walls extended on either bank onto what was now dry land. The stone blockhouses still stood, but empty, abandoned.

"Don't look," David said tersely and pointed away, trying to distract my gaze.

But there was no missing the body of the dwarf. It was impaled on a broken timber that jutted up and out from the ruins. The body was burned black. No way to know if he had been dead before he burned.

I tensed, waiting, expecting a crude joke from Christopher. Something about my being burned at the stake. But nothing.

It was a gruesome sight. And there was more to come. The dwarfs had built a number of gold-panning sluices downstream. These were shattered. Buildings as well, barracks I suppose they were, and storehouses. All wrecked, twisted, flattened, strewn around the wet, muddy landscape like so much garbage. There were bodies here and there, dwarfs, some in chain mail, others in long nightshirts as though they had died while sleeping.

The river curved left around a bare, rocky promontory. The rocks rose twenty feet above us. And there stood a solitary dwarf, alive, weeping into his mud-heavy beard. He blinked at us. Dashed away his tears and shook his fist at us.

"You think you are proud conquerors?" he yelled. "Gloat while you may. Dwarfs do not forget. Every dwarf in Everworld will know of your foul deed. Never stray to the mountains, dwarf-killers. You will be slaves in our deepest mines and die without light!"

No one answered him. David refused to look at him and we all followed suit. Pretended not to see or hear him.

Only when we were out of range of his guttural curses and threats did Christopher say, "Great, we really needed more people trying to kill us."

"We had no choice," Jalil said, trying to convince himself. "Sobek could have attacked us. Maybe the Coo-Hatch would have stopped him, but maybe not. How many crocodiles does he have, after all? They're fast, you know. Crocodiles. They move surprisingly quickly on land."

"It's behind us now," David said tersely.

I wondered whether Sobek had followed us through the breach. Was he still there, gliding beneath the water? I was too worn to use my powers. I was wrung out, limp.

"Yeah, let's forget about it," April said, dripping acid. "We kill a bunch of people, let's just forget about that. Jesus, what are we doing? This place . . . We can't let ourselves . . ." She petered out, unable to frame her maudlin sentiments.

But Jalil couldn't let it go. "We have to reach Egypt, we have to help the Coo-Hatch — if we don't they'll back the Hetwan, the Hetwan will take Olympus, and then it's just a matter of time before Ka Anor wins. Once he has all of Everworld he'll punch his way into the real world. We have to do whatever it takes to win. Or else worse stuff will happen. Far worse."

I said, "What an original thought, Jalil. I wonder if that rationalization has ever been used before? We have to kill to stop the killing. We have to be depraved to stop the depravity. Yeah, I wonder if anyone has ever thought that up before."

Jalil didn't answer, just dug his oars into the water and forced David to counter his ill-timed stroke.

"It's all funny to you, isn't it, Senna?" April said. "It's all a joke. You don't understand the idea of a conscience. Right and wrong is all a big joke to you."

Time for a counterstroke. "Is it? At least I have a plan, April. I could give myself over to Loki and let him break through into the real world. It would be the easy thing to do. But I resist, don't I? I resist and I plan for a better Everworld, an Everworld that is not a threat to the real world."

"Maybe you should let us in on your plan someday," Christopher sneered. "Because as far as I know your plan seems to be to screw over everyone you run into, trash everyone and everything, play everyone against everyone else until you're the only one left standing. Maybe I missed some subtleties."

I hid a smile. *No,* I thought silently, *you have it exactly right.* I felt very good all of a sudden. It was all going to work. I could feel it. How long would it take? Years? Months? It didn't matter.

I knew it. It had worked for me before. After all, Everworld was not the first place I had come to as a stranger, an outcast, a despised intruder.

That first time I had come into a strange, unknown world driven in a limousine, sitting belted in across from the shaken, nervous man who was my father.

It was my first time in a limousine. The driver had raised the privacy glass so my father could talk freely. But my father had very little to say. He bit a thumbnail and looked out of tinted windows at dim streetlights as we sped north from Chicago.

He was a trapped man. I saw that, even then. I knew he was afraid. That reassured me. I was afraid, too. If we were both afraid then he was not greater than I.

I decided not to be afraid. By being unafraid I could be stronger. I knew that intuitively. Or perhaps it was something my mother had taught me, I don't know.

What I knew was that life had changed permanently. My mother was gone. Our world of candlelit apartments, strange visitors, intermittent school, and frequent moves was gone. Done. I could touch the black leather seats of the limousine and understand that much.

My father used the car's phone to call ahead. He'd put some thought into it. Couldn't say too much, couldn't say too little. And he had to watch what he said in front of me. After all, I was just a little girl.

"Honey, something has happened. No, no, I'm not hurt. It's . . . I'm bringing someone home with me. Her name is Senna. She's a little girl." Deep breath. "Honey, she's mine, and I know, I know, and I'm so sorry. But she's just a little girl and —"

I heard the click. His face twitched. He hung up the phone.

We arrived ten minutes later and, knowing he was walking into a hornet's nest, he was suddenly very solicitous of me. Maybe he figured I was his only possible ally.

My stepmother's face was frozen. I could have shattered it into pieces with a hammer, it was so brittle. She looked at me, not angry at me, but angry. Livid. Pained. And guilty?

There was a little girl my own age standing halfway down the steps, in her jammies, holding a stuffed doll.

My stepmother said, "April, this little girl is going to spend the night. Your father and I have to talk. I want you to take her upstairs and show her the guest room. Do that for me, sweetie, that's a good girl."

"Her name is Senna," my father said.

"I don't care!" the woman snapped.

The little girl looked dubiously at me. She had enormous eyes and lush red hair. She was terribly polite. Terribly well-raised. She helped me carry my things.

"This is the guest room in here." She opened the door. It was cold inside. The heating vent had been closed. She snapped on a bedside light. It was a room straight out of a magazine. Unlike anything I'd ever seen in my own experience. The quilt matched the curtains, which picked up a pattern in the wallpaper.

"Who are you?" I asked the girl.

"I'm April. What's your name?"

I thought about it. My name was Senda. But my father had called me Senna. Senda meant "pathway." My mother was always one for languages. It was how she made her way in the world, as a translator. In fact, I'd never thought of it, but she seemed able to understand anything anyone said, regardless of language.

"My name is Senna Wales," I said. Then, wanting to wipe the smug, pitying expression off her little face, I added, "That's what my daddy calls me."

"Where is your daddy?"

"That's him downstairs."

Her eyes clouded. "That's my daddy."

"Not anymore," I said. "Now he's mine. You can keep her."

At that moment the sound of yelling came up through the floor. A loud, shrill female voice overriding a softer, humbled male voice.

"You can still pretend he's your daddy if you want to," I told April. "But you and I will know."

All these years later it gave me shivers, that

memory. I had been a smart little girl. Or at least one with good instincts.

There were two paths I could have followed: Try to fit in, assimilate, join the family, be the good little girl at home and at school — and I would still never, ever fit in.

Or I could dominate them by keeping them off-guard, by manipulating, surprising, disturbing them.

I could be a false part of their Great Big Happy Family, or I could create my own life and live without controls.

They would never love me, no one ever would, my own mother had left me. My own mother didn't . . . Well then, let them be afraid of me.

We paddled and drifted and paddled some more. We were hungry and thirsty, unable to drink from the river that carried the bodies of the dead dwarfs.

On both banks of the river we could see the effects of the dwarfs' dam: fields of sun-blasted, scrawny wheat, trees picked clean, gaunt oxen, shriveled men and women and babies. Famine, or near famine.

They were all smiling now, the myopic stares and gap-toothed grins of the old men, the scared-hopeful Madonna smiles of mothers, the clueless smiles of little children.

They gathered by the riverbank to wave at us, to cry out their thanks. We were the first people to appear from upriver in a long time and we had brought the river back with us. These people had seen the debris of the dam floating by, they'd probably seen bodies. They knew that we had opened the river again and they greeted us as heroes.

A man splashed out to us and handed us a skin of wine which all of us but David passed around gratefully. Another man breasted the waters to press a handful of dates on us. Perhaps the last of his own food.

April was no longer whining about the dead dwarfs. Now she was seeing the other side and, typically, the emotion swayed her. The dwarfs were just as dead but now these people were all happy about it, so . . .

The river wound on through desolate farmlands and past small, mud-brick villages. The people had very little but they gave freely of what they did have. By afternoon we had all the dates, figs, apricots, bread, and yogurt we could eat. All the wine and water we could drink. And palm fronds to protect us from the sun. We were even offered a slave.

"We're rock stars," Christopher said. "We could so totally take advantage of this. Egyptian groupies. Cool. Walk like an Eee-gyptian."

"Maybe we should start looking for a place to spend the night," David said. "Couple more hours, it will be dark and we can't be on the river after dark. Maybe the next village, if we see one. The people don't seem like they'll be any trouble."

We turned a bend in the river, came out of the shadow of a bluff, and all at once were there.

"No way," Christopher said with an incredulous laugh. "Pyramids! That is a pyr-a-freaking-mid! Look at that thing."

The pyramid was the model of every pyramid in every encyclopedia ever written, but without the ravages of the millennia on its face. It was tall, smooth, perfect in its proportions. It might have just been built. Every one of the millions of stones was sharp and clear, as though cut with a razor.

And unlike the modern, real-world picture of a pyramid, it did not rise from barren sand. Rather it was surrounded by well-landscaped, irrigated gardens that seemed especially startling by contrast with the poverty and desolation we had passed through.

It took an hour to reach and then pass by the pyramid. It was farther away than we'd imagined, an optical illusion. And it was huge. We were ten minutes in its shadow.

"Okay, we need to be thinking 'prepared,'" David said. "We don't know, so let's not get lazy." To illustrate his point he loosened his sword in its scabbard.

"What, mummies are gonna swim out here after us?" Christopher mocked.

"Arrows, Christopher. You know, bow and arrow? From the pyramid, from any high point on the riverbank. Anyone sees a bow, yell, duck down below the gunwale."

"The what?"

"The side of the boat," David said with a sigh.

We rowed on and swept at last out of the pyramid's shadow. But now the river carried us between two huge stone sphinxes, one on either bank. Both were painted. Lips red, eyes heavily made up in trailer-trash blue, with the cowl done in turquoise stripes.

They were at once intimidating, overwhelming, and comic.

"Mimi has been here," Christopher said.

"Who?" Jalil asked.

"You need to watch more TV, Jalil. Mimi? On *Drew Carey*?"

We drifted past the sphinxes and David said, "Senna, you have any handy hints on how to deal with these people? These Egyptians?"

I shrugged. "Not really. Try not to get into a confrontation." What was I supposed to say?

Jalil said, "Last time I crossed over I did some research. These guys are highly ritualistic. They don't see any line between religion and ritual and everyday life; it's all one to them. Baking bread is a religious ritual as far as they're concerned, and they do it in exactly the same way every time. Their goal in life is to keep everything the same, year after year, unchanging. These guys make the most ultraconservative you've ever met look like a crazy party animal. If nothing changes for a thousand years, that's cool by them."

"Great. Should be a real party," Christopher said. "They don't do the human sacrifice thing, do they?"

"No. They sacrifice animals and whatnot. And the pharaoh is a god and you don't talk to him or look at him or touch him. If he likes you he'll let you kiss the floor. If he doesn't like you —"

"— then you kiss his ass?" Christopher interjected.

"No, that would be a sign of favor. You wish he liked you well enough to let you kiss his ass. No, I was going to say that these gods, Pharaoh included, are hard-core. You don't argue with them. They don't like you, you die, no questions asked."

"We're not here to shoot the breeze with Pharaoh," David pointed out. "We're here to find Senna's mother. Period."

Christopher laughed. "I hadn't thought about it, but this must be making you kind of nervous, huh, Moses? Hebrews and Egyptians? There's a little history going on there. Here's the thing: We get into any trouble, you'll have to go to Pharaoh and tell him, 'Let my people go.' Of course, you'll need frogs. And locusts."

April laughed. "We'll inflict the plague of you, Christopher. Pharaoh troubles us, we'll send you in to recite all the *Brady Bunch* episodes you've memorized."

Past the sphinxes, the high riverbanks became sheer stone levees rising ten or more feet. Stairways, twenty, thirty steps long descended from the elevated riverbank down into the water, or down to floating wooden platforms. The number of small boats increased suddenly and dramatically. Upstream, the river had been blocked, but here we were nearer the sea, and traffic had continued to move in that direction.

Yet even here it was easy to see the damage done by the destruction of the dam. A number of small boats had been smashed into toothpicks by the sudden surge.

It was increasingly obvious that there were profound differences between the left and right banks of the river. On the left bank were smaller, less ostentatious structures that might have been warehouses. And it was on that bank that larger ships could be seen tied up to the quays. Some of those ships, too, had been mauled by the river's sudden rise. There were masts snapped in half and one large boat had a three-foot hole caved in its side.

But overall the left bank looked to be a pretty cheerful place. Shirtless, loinclothed workers were unloading bales, balancing tremendous loads on sunburned backs, and laughing and singing as they worked.

Beyond the warehouses I saw glimpses of smaller buildings, homes perhaps, businesses. The streets were busy but not bustling. People moved slowly, unhurriedly, some pulling carts, some pushing wheelbarrows, many carrying loads on their heads. The men wore loincloths or simple tunics; the women wore crudely cut dresses, sometimes belted. White linen was the fabric of choice, though here and there splashes of trade goods could be seen, red and indigo scarves, even occasionally an entire sky-blue or spring-green dress.

There were donkeys and cattle in the streets and an occasional horse. Dogs barked. Children yelled in shrill voices. The left bank was alive.

The right bank was a different picture entirely. Here were more elaborate, larger wharves decorated with statuary, but these wharves were mostly empty of boats.

The right bank was home to massive stone structures that could only be temples and palaces. There were massive, sloped porticoes ten times the height of a man and decorated with painted images of gods and goddesses; there were forts with crenelated walls; and looming statues of seated gods, hands on knees, pleated beards, and faces painted in lurid colors.

The left bank was built to human scale. The right bank belittled humans, abashed them, crushed them with its size and the sheer weight of stone on stone on stone.

Very little moved on the right bank. What movement there was, was slow, deliberate. Files of men in white linen skirts and no shirts. Women in sheer linen shifts. All with black wigs, or shaved heads and topknots. These people, these slow, deliberate, indifferent people had the unmistakable look of priests and priestesses.

I swallowed in a dry throat. The right bank. I would find her there. That was the home for a priestess of Isis.

"I'm thinking left bank is for people, right bank for gods," April said. "Let's go left."

"We are looking for the temple of Isis," I reminded her. "That is where we will find my mother."

I sounded calm, but I didn't feel at all calm.

This was a meeting I had so often imagined. How many times had I played this scene out in my head during the last ten years? The naive fantasies of a lonely seven-year-old had matured over time; the words, the scenes, the actions, and reactions had all been rewritten a thousand times. The play had been refined, but the play had never closed. There had seldom been a day, or more often night, when I did not see the moment in my imagination.

And now I might be within minutes of seeing her again. Within minutes of . . . of what? That would be up to her, at first. Over the long term I would decide, but the tone of that first meeting, that would be up to her.

If she was still alive. If she was still here. If.

I took a deep, slow breath. *Keep your balance,* I warned myself. Keep your powers ready; keep your mind clear and alert. Don't be distracted. Let there be no emotion.

"Senna's right," David said. "We need to get in and out of this place ASAP. So we go straight to Mrs. Wales. Tell her what's up, and if she plays ball, we just get the hell out of here. I don't get a good feeling off the right bank."

Ahead on the right was a low stone quay reached by three stairways. There were figures there, hard to make out through the statues and through the masts and rigging of intervening boats, but I saw dull gold reflections of sunlight on bronze. Soldiers. Guards.

"There," David pointed. "I think we're expected."

"I think I see military types," Jalil said.

"Yeah. And if we try and blow past them, they probably won't be too happy. Best go in like we have nothing to hide."

In fact, as we approached, it was clear that there were indeed soldiers, rapidly rushing down to the platform, hurrying to form up into neat rows. Forty, maybe fifty or more.

They wore white kilts, I suppose you'd call them. And nothing else. No shirts, no shoes. They carried spears topped with copper blades and shields that looked as if they were made of wood and cowhide. Some carried bows and a decorated quiver of arrows.

"They don't look too tough," Jalil said under his breath.

"Yeah, but there are a lot of them," David countered.

"They don't look tough," April said, "but *they* do."

"Who?"

She pointed higher. "Them."

Three of them stood atop the high retaining wall, looking down on the Egyptian soldiers on the quay. Each of them was at least six feet tall. Each was armored: steel breastplates decorated with gold and silver, helmets with foot-tall combs of feathers, spiked steel straps at the wrists, massive belts decorated with insignia the size of truckers' belt buckles.

At their sides they wore long swords, like we'd seen the Vikings use. On the other side they wore long knives. Shorter knives protruded from the tops of their worn, knee-high leather boots. Each had a long bow hanging from a strap and a quiver of arrows. And on their left hands they wore a sort of chain-mail half-glove with a row of sharp talons protruding from the back of the hand. And then there were the coiled bullwhips.

They were hard, muscled, scarred, snarling warriors. And they were women.

They had the easy swagger of conquerors. The wide stance of natural rulers. One tipped up a jar, let wine dribble down her chin, and then spit a mouthful out in a spray over the flinching soldiers below.

She laughed and her friends laughed and slapped her on the back.

"Are those Egyptians?" David asked me, incredulous.

"I don't know what those are," I admitted. I was worried. This was an unforeseen development. To put it mildly.

"I think I read about those chicks," Christopher said under his breath. "May have been in a letter to *Penthouse*."

I hadn't really noticed, but the women had one other notable feature: Beneath the snarls, the scars, the weapons, the armor, they were each beautiful.

"We've come to Planet Dominatrix," Christopher said. "If I'd known, hell, I'd have hurried more. I swear that's Heidi Klum with a whip."

David said, "You really think those ladies look like they want to hear your jokes? Look at the Egyptians, man. They're cowering there. They have copper speartips, for God's sake, copper."

"Yeah, copper, so what?"

"The ladies have steel. Steel is to copper what a meat cleaver is to Velveeta. You got forty guys down here on the platform all taking abuse from those three. So maybe this isn't the time for your little sex fantasies."

As if to emphasize the point, an Egyptian official of some sort passed the three armored women. He was dressed in blazing white linen and wore a magnificent cowl headdress. He was attended by a half-dozen acolytes, young men with shaved heads and knots of black hair protruding from the side of their heads.

The man in the cowl was clearly someone important. But as he and his party passed, one of the viragos grabbed an acolyte and fondled him in the crudest possible way.

Another of the women loosened her whip, waited till the Egyptian official was past, whirled the leather overhead, and snapped it. The man jumped and yelped in pain, all dignity lost.

The three women then laughed uproariously. But their smiles never reached their eyes, which were narrowed, focused, aimed right at us. They were putting on a show for our benefit. Letting us know that they were in charge.

The official recovered as best he could and met us as we docked our boats. David started to jump out, but the shocked expression on the face of the official or priest or whatever he was stopped David in midstep.

"I am the humble mouth of great King Ankhahut, the twelfth of that name. I am come to welcome you to the City of the Sun."

"Glad to —"

"I welcome you in the name of Ra, the creator, Khnum-Ra, Amon-Ra, Harakhti-Ra, Meren-Ra, Menthu-Ra . . ."

For the next five minutes we stood there, frozen, unwilling to give offense, as the man named the names and attributes of various Ra's. Five endless minutes and he was clearly still early in the recitation.

"How many gods do they have?" Christopher muttered to Jalil.

"At this rate? Probably several hours' worth."

David sent me a helpless look. Waiting for me to suggest a course of action. But the women warriors intervened and saved us the effort.

One of them swaggered down to the platform, pushed her way through the unprotesting soldiers, and said, "Come on. This damned fool will go on like this forever. Ra this and Ra that and Ra my fundament. Ra is a cobweb-covered half-corpse sitting in a dusty hole mewling like a kitten."

She reached and grabbed David and half-dragged him, half-lifted him onto solid ground. She leered at him, pushing her face close to his. "So. You'd be the ones who sent those dwarfs swimming this morning. Well, you've made trouble, that's for sure, but it was damned fine soldiering. For a man. You look like you could be a spirited ride, eh? Eh, my little stallion?"

And then she grabbed David in a way that made him gasp. "I am Merope. Princess Merope," she added, as if daring anyone to disagree. And while she still had him, she shot a look at April. "Is he yours?"

"What? No."

"He's mine," I said.

Merope released David reluctantly and gave me a dirty look. "May he give you sons," she spat, obviously a curse. "How about this one?" She jerked a thumb at Christopher.

"Oh, I'm available," Christopher said brightly.

"You're tall," the woman said. "That's good. But you'll be a few inches shorter by the time I'm done with you."

"Hey!" she cried over her shoulder to her companions. "Did you hear that? I said it was good he was tall because he'd be a few inches shorter by the time I'm finished with him!"

The other two laughed, although with the

forced sound of people who've heard a particular joke before.

"Come on," Merope said, poking Christopher with the braided leather handle of her whip. "I'll take you to see the boss."

"The Pharaoh?" April asked.

Merope barked a laugh. "The Pharaoh? That bloodless, drooling, inbred sister's husband? No, my sweet innocent, we go to see Pretty Little Flower, the queen of all the Amazons. She rules in Egypt."

"Amazons?" Christopher mouthed silently.

Just then, a cry and a splash. One of the soldiers had made a break for it. He had broken ranks, rushed to the edge, and leaped into the water. He was swimming now, badly, ineptly, flailing and thrashing in the muddy water.

On the far bank a few people gathered and pointed. Some cheered encouragingly. Others seemed to be placing bets. One of the men actually yanked down his loincloth and mooned us.

The soldier was halfway across when Merope unlimbered her bow. She was in no hurry. "There's no sport unless he makes it halfway first," she explained.

But the soldier wouldn't be making it that far. He screamed, surprised, horrified. The water boiled around him, he screamed again and again, Merope and the Amazons frowned.

In seconds it was all over. The crocodiles had done their work.

"That will discourage the others," one of the Amazons said darkly.

Merope suddenly drew her bow and let fly. An arrow arced above the water. The man who had been mooning us had pulled up his loincloth, but that didn't stop the arrow from suddenly sprouting from his upper thigh.

The Amazons burst into laughter and shouted obscene threats across the water as the shot man was attended to by friends who moved him (and themselves) quickly out of range.

"Well, come along," Merope said. "That's all the fun for now."

I looked back as we climbed the stairs leading up to the street level and saw the official. He was still speaking; he had never stopped, never hesitated. He was still reciting the names of all the welcoming gods. Talking away to the empty space where we had stood. And his acolytes and remaining soldiers all stood at attention, expressionless, seemingly indifferent to the fact that we were no longer there, indifferent even to the horrible fate of their companion.

The ritual was being observed.

Chapter XV

Merope and her two friends marched us through the imposing stone gateway and into the city. They swaggered on ahead, apparently not concerned that we would run away or disappear.

Massive buildings, columns painted with hieroglyphs and stylized portraits of the gods, rose on either side of the dusty street. The style was different from the Greeks'. The Greeks achieved a certain delicacy, even in the largest structures. But these temples seemed to have been made out of the largest stones anyone could find, all piled together to create massive slabs. It was a statement of size, not grace, sheer weight, not soaring ambition.

There were no businesses, no shops. There were no horses or mules or even camels in the streets.

None of the activity that was to be found over on the left bank of the Nile. No one walked the streets at all, but for an occasional file of priests or priestesses, moving along, heads down, no doubt focused on some necessary ritual.

Some priests wore cowls, others displayed a shaved head, others still wore head-covering masks made to represent wolves or dogs of some kind. They wore wraparound linen skirts, or kilts, occasionally a beaded collar.

The priestesses wore white linen shifts, almost transparent in the slanting sunlight. They wore identical black Cleopatra wigs, sometimes bound with gold headbands.

They walked in files of five or ten priests or priestesses, carrying gold censers full of burning incense, the sweet-sickly smell of which made me want to gag whenever I caught a full whiff. My mother had always favored incense.

But for long stretches there weren't even any of these oppressed creatures. Just emptiness. Silence. Silence compounded by the abashing mass of stone and frozen-pose paintings.

"What is this, Planet of the Zombies?" April wondered. "This place gives me the creeps. There's no noise."

"Look, kitties!" Jalil said.

"Kitties?" Christopher repeated. "Did you just say 'kitties'?"

"Cats. I said cats," Jalil amended. "Look, there, by that doorway."

At least a dozen cats lounged comfortably on a slab of sun-warmed stone beside a doorway that could have easily admitted a dinosaur.

"Hey, look, there are more up there." April pointed. "And there. Jeez. A lot of cats."

They were easy to overlook at first in the shadow of skyscraper slabs of stone. But once noticed, they seemed to be everywhere.

"Anyone ever see *The Birds*? All these seagulls go nuts and start killing people?" Christopher asked nervously. "These kitties look like bad kitties."

April laughed. "There's no such thing as a bad kitty. Didn't the ancient Egyptians treat them like gods? Here, kitty. Here, kitty, kitty."

Jalil said, "You know, watch what you say. They may be able to talk."

"W.T.E.," Christopher agreed. "Welcome To Everworld."

April diverted toward a cluster of cats in the shadow of a stone lion. Then she stopped, froze, and let go with a scream that jerked the Amazons around, swords at the ready.

Merope was in full combat mode and David not a split second behind her. Then Merope laughed. "Oh, that." She sheathed her sword and shook her head in amused contempt.

April rejoined us, shaken, white-faced, hands wringing.

"What was it?" David demanded, still not sure he should relax.

"The cats. They were . . . There's a dead person over there. The cats are eating him."

"Not much else to eat," Merope said philosophically. "The Nile stopped up, the farmlands half barren, and the rebels over on the left bank aren't sending much food this way. Godless, motherless sons of dogs."

"You can't just leave a dead man in the streets to be eaten by cats!" April yelled.

Merope shrugged. "It was his choice. He fathered twin boys on Oriana there."

Oriana, the blond Amazon, nodded. "And he was a poor gallop at that. No heart. Like riding a sick gelding."

They all laughed at that picture.

"He was no loss, and when his time came he chose to feed the cats. A lot of them go that way. They don't have the things they need to make mummies anymore, you know, not for most of them. No way to reach the Afterworld, so they feed the cats and hope for the best. Of course, now the cats have the taste in their mouths." She shook her head regretfully. "It's only a good thing they don't hunt in packs, the little monsters, or we'd none of us be left alive."

We set off again, but with all of my companions casting nervous glances at the cats we saw. As though that were the problem. As though we had to fear a plague of cats.

Egypt was dead. At least this part of the city, the right bank. It was dead, mummified. And the Amazons ruled. That much was clear. What was not clear was what this meant for me.

I wondered if my mother was here, could she still be here? To come all this way and . . . All the years I had remembered her words. *Look for me with Mother Isis.*

Look for me with Mother Isis. For so long I hadn't even known what the words meant. Then one day I happened to be at the mall.

I was perhaps thirteen. I had sprouted up, grown tall and thin. I was beginning to fill out, as my stepmother called it. She had taken me aside to warn me that boys would start looking at me with more than casual interest. And she'd told me that I would probably find my own desires growing stronger. I would have to learn to fight that part of me. It was bad and wrong and would lead to trouble.

I remember wondering if she had offered April the identical dire warning. I later learned she had, but in modified form. April, you see, was her daughter. I was the daughter of the slut who had seduced her husband. April's instruction in sex did not include the possibility that she might be inclined to encourage all those terrible boys.

In any event, I was at the mall, walking around with my stepmother's words still fresh in mind, watching the boys who passed, wondering what this new power might mean. Wondering whether it was a fearful threat or an opportunity.

And I happened to notice a boy, a young man, really. He may have been seventeen or eighteen. He looked at me, watched me till I felt his eyes on me. I did not blush, did not turn away. I met his gaze and he didn't look away, either. For a long moment we simply looked into each other's eyes from a distance of twenty feet, looking past the shoppers who crossed between us.

He was attractive, I suppose. But that was not what made me stare. He had the glow.

Then he turned slowly and walked into the Museum Shop. And I followed. He had the glow. I had not seen it since my mother. I had felt it, known it was in me, but had not seen it till this moment, and I knew deep down that it was no accident.

He moved confidently, knowing I would follow. I kept my distance. Not sure how this game was played.

He moved along the wall, past the lighted displays of framed reproductions, past the games, past the Frank Lloyd Wright stained glass. Then he stopped in front of a display case of objects done in gold leaf.

He stopped and I stopped. He looked a long time, and I could not see what he was looking at. Then he moved on.

I went and stood where he had stood and looked at what he had seen. And there she was, a plaster figure in gold leaf and enamel paint, golden wings spread wide.

A little card said, *Isis*.

The boy with the glow was gone. I never saw him again.

For a while I wondered if my mother had simply gone to Egypt, modern Egypt. But I knew that wasn't it. My mother was somewhere, somewhere strange and impossible to reach. And she was with the winged goddess.

Now I was here, in the land that Ra and Isis and the other gods were supposed to rule.

I watched as a file of priestesses shuffled past, eyes blank, wreathed in a foul cloud of incense. They prayed as they went, mouthing words, repeating, repeating lines they'd said a million times. They didn't even look at us.

Could my mother possibly be alive in this mausoleum? By all the powers, could anyone be said to be alive in this land of living death?

Pretty Little Flower was not on her throne when we came in. In fact, she was doing the last thing any of us would have expected. She was singing to an admiring gaggle of Amazons who lounged, but respectfully, as their supreme leader used her rather lovely voice to belt out the instantly recognizable lyrics.

"R-E-S-P-E-C-T, that is what it means to me, R-E-S-P-E-C-T, take care of —"

She stopped when she saw us and glared angrily. Merope recoiled a step before that murderous expression.

"I did not know, Highness!" Merope stammered. "There were no guards at the door, no . . ."

Pretty Little Flower chopped the air impatiently, cutting off the explanation. "I was not in voice, anyway. I failed to do justice to the Goddess Aretha. What are these creatures?"

Pretty Little Flower was not quite what either her name implied or what one thought of as an Amazon. For a start she was no Greek. No type of Mediterranean at all. Perhaps Chinese, perhaps Japanese, maybe Korean, but with a mix of African and Caucasian thrown in for good measure.

She was tall, like all the Amazons. Slender, lovely, and strange. Blue eyes, skin the color of a lion's mane, hair that was straight, full, and jet-black. She wore a fantastic breastplate covered with intricate scrollwork in gold and silver. It was narrow at the waist but rose in a V to form bright steel eagle claws that seemed to protect her shoulders without hampering her movements.

At her waist she wore a curved sword, a scimitar, with an impressively bejeweled hilt, in a scabbard paved with tiny rubies. She, too, carried a whip. And a small throwing disc I had seen before.

Her muscular legs were encased in knee-high boots of supple fawn leather. There was a half-moon of small steel barbs projecting from the toes of her boots.

She moved with the grace and ease of an athlete or ballet dancer, always perfectly balanced, always in control of every ounce of her lean body. I saw her as a leopard, a sinuous, beautifully dangerous predator.

"Michelle Kwan meets Tyra Banks," Christopher muttered under his breath. Quiet but not quiet enough.

The disc was in her hand and flying before I became conscious of the slightest movement. Even then it was barely a ripple, barely a disturbance in her impressive physical calm. The disc flew.

Christopher cried out in pain and slapped his hand to his cheek. The disc circled back to the queen and she caught it without so much as looking at it.

A Coo-Hatch throwing disc.

A bright red line had been drawn in Christopher's cheek. A superficial cut.

"Don't worry, big boy, it won't leave a scar," she said. "But now you will remember: A man does not speak to me unless invited. A little rule of mine."

Christopher nodded, silent.

"See? You remembered," she said pleasantly. She patted him on his good cheek and gave it a squeeze. "There's a good boy. Merope, explain your interruption."

"Yes, Highness. These are the ones who destroyed the dwarfs' dam. They arrived in boats. We brought them straight here. I did not realize Your Highness was singing."

"We're past that," the queen said, smiling to herself, amused at Merope's clumsy sincerity. "So. You're the ones." She looked us over carefully, one by one.

"You would be the warrior here?" she asked David. "Let me see your sword."

David is no fool. He drew his sword slowly, carefully, using just two fingers, and handed the hilt to her.

Pretty Little Flower burst out laughing and all the Amazons joined in. "You are a wise one."

She hefted the sword and swung it in a series of slashing moves, over her head, down low, a figure eight at blinding speed. The blade halted a hair away from David's neck. He didn't flinch.

"No coward," she admitted reluctantly. "And this is a very fine sword. The balance is impeccable. The steel is very good as well. I would say . . . Old World. English, Welsh perhaps. Made in the style of the old Druids, and certainly enchanted. A very old sword." She peered at David through narrowed eyes. "Not yours."

"Mine now," David said. "It was the sword of Galahad."

"My father?" a voice yelped in distress. One of the Amazons. An olive-skinned blond with alarming pale eyes.

"Galahad's sword?" Pretty Little Flower demanded. "Ah, there was a great man. He was very nearly a woman. I mourn his passing. A dragon, I suppose?"

"Yes," David said. "He was badly wounded fighting Loki and an army of trolls. In the end, he was unable to resist the dragon that killed him."

Pretty Little Flower handed the sword back to David and in a casual voice said, "I allow you to keep it, but you understand that if you should budge that sword as much as an inch from its scabbard you will die instantly?"

David nodded and sheathed the sword. "Your own sword is of an unusual shape," he said, and then winced in realization that he had addressed her without being invited.

Pretty Little Flower flared, teeth bared, then relented. "It is also of Old World design," she said. "Damascus steel. The shape is called a scimitar. It is better for close-in work, easier to draw when on horseback. It has several advantages."

I noticed David eyeing the Coo-Hatch throwing disc. So did the queen.

"Ah, you recognize this weapon, then?"

"We know the Coo-Hatch."

"A morose race, but ah, such metal-workers! If we had a hundred Coo-Hatch blades we would rule all of Everworld, not just all of Egypt."

This caused laughs and self-congratulatory babble from the appreciative audience.

Pretty Little Flower ignored all that and stared hard at me. "What are you?"

"A woman," I said.

A faint smile. "No." She pointed at April. "She is a woman, she fears me. These are men, they fear me. You do not fear me. You carry no weapons, you are not strong, not swift. So why do you not fear me?" It was a rhetorical question. I didn't volunteer an answer. "You are a witch."

Still I didn't answer. But I prepared. I gathered the power into me, held it in readiness. If she moved I would strike. I stood poised, confident, prepared.

Pretty Little Flower laughed, much amused. Her laughter was not a bluff, and that worried me. She should be worried, and she wasn't. I felt the first thin trickle of fear.

"This one would be a queen," Pretty Little Flower said. "She has the thirst for power. So frail, so weak. She must be very sure of her powers."

Still, I had no answer. What could I say? Anything I said would be wrong.

"Let's go eat!" she said suddenly. "I feel my voice returning. Let us eat and drink and I will sing to the goddess Aretha and the goddess Joni and the goddess Madonna."

Where had the queen of the Amazons learned about Aretha? I could guess the answer.

It was one of my memories of my mother. She was the clichéd, hippie wanna-be, my mother was. She was too young, hadn't really been there for the sixties. But she favored flowered muumuu dresses and beads and candles everywhere.

And her friends, when she had them at all, were of a similar type. Women who thought they became witches by dreaming up a sort of religion. They called it Wicca. It was harmless enough, no doubt. Women would come over to our apartment and chant and sing and talk about "the goddess."

I would be asleep by then, at least in theory. But I've never needed much sleep. So I would sit in my "room," which was nothing more than an alcove of our living room, closed off at night by drawing a Madras-print cotton tablecloth across a stretched rope.

I could see through the fabric, could make out the glow of candles, the bright happy faces. And of course I could hear the talk, the poetry, the songs, the chants. And smell the incense, the pot, and the wine.

I could see that my mother glowed and the others did not. I knew that she knew that they were not what we were. They were not freaks of nature, they were just people. And what we were, we two, had nothing to do with chanting or incense or prayers to a "goddess."

But I suppose my mother was lonely. I suppose she needed friends. People do, it seems.

I would lie there, blankets up to my chest, on my side, head on my hand, and listen and watch through the tablecloth, like watching a movie on a blurred screen.

As the night wore on they grew more stoned, drunker. And then the solemn chants would be replaced by less pious music. The women would put on a CD — a record then, I guess — and sing along and even stand up and perform dance moves.

R-E-S-P-E-C-T.

Yes, my mother still lived.

CHAPTER XVII

Pretty Little Flower led the way from her throne room through a space whose purpose I could not imagine since it seemed to be filled with nothing but bulbous pillars covered entirely with bright picture-stories of the various gods.

But after a while we were through that pillar maze, the Amazons laughing and joking and playing grab-ass with Christopher and now Jalil. We passed through a slab-sided portal and then through more rows of columns and finally into an open courtyard. Night had fallen fully. The sky was filled with stars.

More columns. Back beneath the roof again and now we entered a narrow room, quite long, dark, and gloomy. The walls were covered with more drawings in the stiflingly stylized Egyptian mode. At the far end of the room was a stone platform.

There was a sense of age, a musty smell, a funereal smell. But if the room was cobwebbed I didn't see any. I peered ahead, trying to see what was at the end of the room, on that platform.

A dozen priestesses stood in neat rows before the stone altar. They chanted something, it was a low murmur, impossible to make out the words. Dim oil lamps lit the creature who rested atop the platform. The amber light shone dully on her folded wings of gold.

Isis. A statue? An idol? She did not move. But surely it was too real to be a mere statue.

"There is Egypt," Pretty Little Flower announced with a contemptuous laugh. "Look at her: great Isis. A goddess. Covered in dust. She sits there day after day, year after year. What does she do? Nothing. Nothing at all. Just listens to the prayers, the chants, watches the incessant rituals. She observes, that's what she does, old Isis."

This speech seemed to be made for my benefit. If Pretty Little Flower expected to shock me, then she was successful. It was Isis. Not a statue, but the goddess herself. Her face still beautiful, unchanged. More exotic, more compelling than the plaster face in the Museum Shop, but nearly as devoid of life.

The priestesses went on with their ritual, ignoring us, backs to us, caring nothing for anything but the ritual, the ritual.

"You come to Egypt and what do you find, eh?" the Amazon queen asked me. "You come looking for what? For Ra? For Osiris? For Isis? Well, they're all here. They are all still alive, still gods, still possessed of all their powers, and yet it is Pretty Little Flower who rules Egypt. Worship death and you become death. And if you want your ass kissed from sunrise to sunrise then you have to hold your ass very still."

I wasn't sure if I was supposed to laugh. She had summarized the fate of the Egyptian pantheon. Crudely but, I suspected, accurately.

"There are no gods in Egypt anymore," Pretty Little Flower said with self-satisfied condescension. "Not here in the city anyway; some of the far-flung minor deities are still alive and alert, yes. But here I rule."

"I see that," I said.

Pretty Little Flower grinned and said, "Come, my witch. Come with me."

I thought she was talking to me. Assumed it. But one of the priestesses took a step back, out of her place, and turned.

The face . . . Older. Thinner. Familiar, yet not. A face I had expected to see and which despite everything, despite all the expectation, left me strangely unmoved.

I didn't run to my mother. Nor she to me. I looked at her. She looked at me. I could not see her feelings, could not tell what emotion hid behind her mask, and I knew she could do no better with me.

"Is that your mother?" April asked me. Her voice was shaky. She was more upset than I was.

Pretty Little Flower whipped her head from face to face. Her narrow eyes narrowed further. "I should have seen it. The mother. The daughter. Yes, of course."

And now, at last, Pretty Little Flower was worried, and I knew why. She'd been unafraid of my magic because she had my mother as her guardian. My mother was her bodyguard against the powers of witches. But now the Amazon queen saw the possibility that her protector was my ally.

In a level voice she said, "Devera, Merope, Aiyana, Eirica, bows."

The four named Amazons unlimbered their bows and fitted arrows in a heartbeat.

"If I seem to falter, if there is any magic done here, kill the two witches. Do not hesitate, and do not wait for my order — they may stop my tongue. While these witches are in my presence you will not put away your arrows even upon my direct orders." Pretty Little Flower made a grim smile and said to me, "You and your mother may have great powers, my little witch, but an arrow well-aimed will still stop your heart."

Pretty Little Flower gave Merope a slight nod and all four arrows flew. I gasped. Not at us! Not at me. All four arrows flew and all four arrows entered Isis' left eye.

For the first time the chanting faltered.

Isis never moved. The arrows stuck out of her eye for a moment, then dissolved and disappeared.

The four Amazons had long since fitted new arrows into their bows and were taking aim at my mother and me.

Pretty Little Flower clapped her hands, a businesslike "let's move on" gesture. "Well, I was going to have everyone join me for a night of food, wine, and sacred song, but I'm sure a mother and daughter have much to say to each other. Merope, take your warriors, escort these witches to the side chamber. Watch them. If they attempt to escape, kill them. As for everyone else, we're having barbecue!"

The queen, her warriors, and my companions all trooped off. David sent me a silent question, and I nodded, releasing him from his duty to protect me. I would be safe. As safe as any of them, anyway.

Merope and her fellow archers walked us to a small room off the courtyard. And there, amid stacks of linen dresses and clay pots of oil, I spoke with my mother for the first time in ten years.

"So. You came," she said.

"I wasn't given much choice."

"Yes, I know. Loki's efforts did not go unnoticed. But you escaped. I'm sure there's a story there. Loki is very dangerous, very clever . . . for a god."

At that point the conversation ground to a halt. This was it? We were to stand awkwardly in a musty little room, sounding like strangers who strike up a desultory conversation while waiting for a bus?

"How have you been, Senda?"

"I go by Senna now," I said.

She frowned. "Senna? That's the name of a tree. The bark is used for medicines. Mostly for laxatives."

"Yes. Fortunately the kids at school don't spend a lot of time reading dictionaries."

She looked down at the floor. "How have you been?"

"How have I been? For the last ten years after you dumped me off? How have I been, the only one like me stuck in a world full of deaf, dumb, and blind fools? Fine, Mom. Fine. How have you been?!"

She shrugged, looked over her shoulder, looked back at the floor. "Not quite what I expected it to be," she said ruefully.

I wanted to laugh. It was absurd. How were we supposed to talk? What were we supposed to do, discuss the last decade of my life and hers?

"You came looking for me," she said after a while. "I appreciate that."

"It's not what you think," I said. I didn't know how much to tell her. I was confused. All my neat scenarios were out the window now, forgotten. My brain was a jumble of bits and pieces: plans, schemes, resentments, desires. Shouldn't she at least try to hug me, put her arms around me?

She looked up, met my gaze for the first time. We were not alike, despite what Pretty Little Flower had said. Maybe our eyes were the same. But her hair was dark, her skin olive. She was shorter than I.

"I didn't know any other way," she said, and her voice broke. "I felt powers watching me, searching for me. I felt them from across the barrier, and I knew they were finding resonant humans they could use to watch me. What happened to you — Fenrir, Loki — it would have happened to me. They would have dragged me across and then used me as a gateway."

"So instead you left me behind as bait," I snapped.

"No! The two of us together, we couldn't help but attract them. I knew the best place to hide was here, in Everworld, although I never knew what it was, or what it was called, back then. I just thought if they can find me in the real world I'll fool them, I'll cross over, I'll hide right under their noses."

"Like I said: with me stuck back there. Not even knowing, having no one to ask, what the hell was I supposed to do?"

She looked blank and shrugged. "I thought . . . I thought maybe they wouldn't find you."

I shook my head. "What? What is that supposed to mean?"

"I was scared, Senda. I was scared. I could feel them, and what was I going to do? I . . . I wasn't doing very well, you know? I could barely make a living. Those awful apartments. Translating, when I could find a job, and you know, all the regular jobs would mean being in an office. I was down to telling fortunes at fairs and . . . You know, men and . . . I was lost, I was . . . I was scared," she finished lamely.

"You just ran away, didn't you?" I said, not even angry. "Lousy apartments? Lousy job? You ran away because you couldn't cope. With life, or with me. So you dumped me off in suburbia and you disappeared."

She made a pained face. A self-pitying face. "I never fit in. I had no place in that world. But I thought if you lived with Tom and his wife, well, maybe, you know . . . a normal school and family vacations and all that. I'll bet you have your own car — Tom was always generous and he made a good living."

I wanted to scream. It was insane. It was incredible, bizarre. The story of my life was about her not making enough money? That was it? With all the bull she'd fed my father, she just wanted to run away so she wouldn't have to get a job?

I took a deep breath, tried to slow the spinning in my head. I pressed my hands against my temples. I was an inconvenience, that was the basic truth. Oh yes, all the rest of it, oh yes, she had felt the pressure of the powers who sought a gateway, but that was more of an excuse than an explanation. She'd been afraid of Loki, of all the predatory gods, but that wasn't the truth of it, that was the gloss on the truth. The truth was that she was just a loser, a misfit, a selfish woman looking for an easier life.

"I . . . I was afraid of you," I admitted, laughing at my own stupidity. "I had this whole thing built up in my mind. You were . . . you were this great woman, this powerful witch, you were this . . . I didn't know what to expect. I saw you in my mind as some high priestess of this powerful goddess. And now? Isis is just a . . . a stump! And this place is a graveyard, overrun by those Amazons."

My mother looked wounded. "Isis was great, once. It's just that they're very old, you know. Much older than the Greeks or the Romans or the Aztecs. Isis had been worshiped for a thousand years before Zeus was even born. And the people, her people, the ritual became an end in itself. The gods here withdrew, further and further into observance, into the rites and ceremonies. The people and the gods together, they just spiraled down and down. Now the Pharaoh, you should see him: He's twenty-nine and has the mind of a four-year-old. He's kept in diapers. Inbreeding, generations of inbreeding. The last twelve Pharaohs have been severely retarded, deformed. This is a civilization that has fallen in on itself, collapsed, turned inward. What power is left was exercised by the vizier. He sent emissaries around Everworld, seeking help, asking for other gods to come and assume control, order an end to the rituals. The priests might listen to a god, he thought. But no help came. Instead there was the rebellion of the people over on the left bank, and the dwarfs dammed the Nile, and the city starved, and then the Amazons came. They are systematically looting this entire civilization, removing the gold and silver from the tombs, carting off everything of value."

"So now you serve the Amazons," I said. "You pray to Isis and go through the motions, but you work for Pretty Little Flower."

My mother grabbed my arm. "She'll get me out of here. She'll get me out of this purgatory, this mausoleum. And don't you screw it up, either. Do you understand me, don't you screw this up for me!"

I pried her fingers off. She had a feral look, a caged animal, trapped, terrified of missing a chance to escape.

"You're pathetic," I said.

She blinked. Took a step back. "I know I haven't been a very good mother to you, Senda. But —"

"It's Senna!" I screamed, so loud that the Amazons nearly loosed their arrows. "That's the name I've lived with, that's the name I have. You dumped me like some bad first date. And now after all this time all you can do is complain. It's all still just you, you, you."

She was confused. Unable to quite grasp what I was saying. So far from being a real mother to me that she could only peer at me, half curious, half afraid, not knowing quite exactly what was bothering me.

I took a deep breath, several. My heart was going so fast I couldn't seem to get air, I felt like the walls were closing in. I wanted to hit her, scratch her, anything to get her to simply feel what I felt, feel what she had done to me.

Pointless. It didn't matter to her. I didn't matter to her. I never had. I never had mattered.

Okay. Okay, then. No more guilt. I was on my own, the way I liked it. On my own and she would realize what I had become, she would realize what I was, who I really was. Now, not years ago, a crying, lost little girl without her mother, no, that was all dead and buried now. It had been for a long time.

I was me, I was Senna Wales, and Pretty Little Flower would serve me, not the other way around. I was —

My mother brushed tears from my eyes with her finger. I slapped her hand away.

"Too late. Way too late."

She looked down at the ground, self-pitying, aggrieved, the injured one. "Did you come here to hurt me?" she asked pitiably.

"No. I came here to use you." Perfect. I delivered the line with cold precision. "I need a gateway. The Coo-Hatch want out of Everworld, and you, Mother, you are going to get them out."

I rejoined the others. Pretty Little Flower was singing "Material Girl," while her Amazons sat cross-legged on the floor or propped on low stools, swaying to the music, seemingly enraptured.

Christopher was enraptured, too, but for other reasons. His face was shining with the effort of keeping so many good jokes all bottled up inside. He was going to burst if he couldn't say something about the wild Amazon queen singing Madonna songs to her flock.

April actually seemed to be enjoying it. She spent her Everworld life with three guys and a half sister she hated. April is a group person, a belonger. In the real world she lived in a cocoon of friends and admirers who all said the same things, and believed the same things, and felt the same way about the same things. The silly cow actually felt at home with the Amazons, like they were just some new clique that had welcomed her.

Jalil watched. Of course Jalil watched. His slitted eyes roamed over the gloomily lit hieroglyphs, always trying to understand.

David was tense. I could see it in his back and neck, in the way he held himself, ready to spring up and draw his sword. As if he had a prayer of surviving a fight.

I made my way to sit with them, excusing myself like someone who comes in late for a movie. I sat between April and David.

"How did it go?" April asked, keeping one eye on Pretty Little Flower, preparing to applaud.

"Well, I learned a lot," I said.

The creature actually put a comforting hand on my arm. She gave me one of her comforting looks. Amazing.

I leaned close to whisper in her ear. "They kill the boy babies. You know that, right? The Amazons. They get pregnant, if it's a girl it lives, if it's a big strong girl it becomes one of them. The weaker ones they sell off as slaves. And the boys? They take them and abandon them in the forest or the mountains or the desert. Enjoy the show."

I was gratified by her look of horror. I was in a foul, dangerous mood, I'll admit that. And wiping the smug, pitying look off April's face made me feel just a bit better.

"What'd your mom say?" David asked me, talking out of the side of his mouth.

"She won't do it."

"Why?"

I laughed. "Because she's a scared, selfish, small woman, that's why." Then, in response to his surprised expression, I added, "If she opens a gateway, Loki will know. He'll come here. He and possibly others. Ka Anor, possibly."

He considered that. Then, surprised, "But you knew that, didn't you?"

I said nothing. I applauded Pretty Little Flower, who now launched into a weird Judy Garland impression singing "Somewhere Over the Rainbow." No song more recent than ten years old, many much older. The Amazons' queen-singer was stuck in a time warp, playing the golden oldies of my mother's day with an emphasis on Carole King, Bonnie Raitt, and Motown.

"There may be trouble," I said to David.

"What kind?" His mouth was set, eyes mean.

"She may tell Pretty Little Flower why we're here. The Amazons are emptying Egypt of everything they can carry away. They're very smart, the Amazons are. Very dangerous. They've become the professional thieves of Everworld. They prey on the weak, and no one is weaker than the Egyptians."

He nodded very slightly. "Your own mother would set you up?"

"She's tied to the Amazons now. She wants out. She wants to get away. They can use her as their priestess for this new religion she's invented for them. They can use her for her powers. They are often generous with other women."

"And with men?"

I smiled. "Paper cups."

"Say what?"

"Use them, throw them away."

A big round of applause and the show was over. Pretty Little Flower accepted the congratulations of her followers/admirers.

The Amazon queen strode, flushed with self-satisfaction, through the milling after-concert crowd. Straight over to us. Straight to April. She jerked her thumb at Christopher.

"Yours?"

Christopher shook his head at April.

"No," April said. "Um, this one is mine." She put her arm around a startled Jalil.

"You must let me borrow him sometime," the queen leered. She took Christopher's hand and led him, totally unprotesting, from the room to the raucous cheers of her warriors.

Merope conducted us out of the temple, down a darkened, abandoned street to a guarded house. We were given rooms and food and even privacy.

But we were also shown the four bored Amazons who took up guard duty outside the door.

"You are honored guests," Merope said with a surly grin. "You freed the Nile and destroyed the dwarfs' dam. Honored guests indeed. And Her Highness would be very disappointed if you were to leave. Her Highness is not a good woman to disappoint, as your blond friend may learn."

She laughed, the others laughed, and we got the message. If we stepped outside of the house we would die.

"So, how screwed are we?" Jalil demanded as soon as we were alone.

"Pretty screwed," David admitted. "Senna's mom won't do it. Worse yet, we figured Senna's mom would be someone who was in tight with the local gods, could give us some cover. Well, I guess she's working for Pretty Little Flower."

"So is Christopher right about now," Jalil said mordantly.

David didn't condescend to respond. "Anyone have any brilliant ideas? Because we could use some. The Amazons are good. You can see it in the way they handle themselves and their weapons. They run this place."

"Mmm," Jalil said, nodding. "Perfect case study. One culture closes in on itself, inbreeds, tries to achieve stasis, shuts out anything new and foreign. Another culture interbreeds, picks up whatever it can technologically, travels, moves from place to place grabbing the best and incorporating it into their culture. I mean, look at how the Amazons have adopted the Aretha religion, or whatever you want to call it. I'm not one to praise any religion, but man, in a straight-up choice between mumbling rituals all day long and singing some decent music while you curl up with a nice glass of wine . . ."

David nodded. "Pretty Little Flower has a Coo-Hatch weapon. And good quality steel. The Egyptians have copper and brass. The level of training is obviously different. Education."

"Oh, shut up, both of you," April snapped. "They're beautiful women with bare legs and big bazooms. The two of you, the three! Christopher, look at him. You're not seeing straight."

"Bazooms?" Jalil mocked.

"Start thinking, David. With your head, for a change. They're child-killers. They're thieves. And how many are there? There can't be more than thirty or forty of them in the city. This is a big city and there are three dozen of them and they're cocky and arrogant."

"They are better armed, better trained than we are, and outnumber us at least six to one," David said. "And by the way, they should be arrogant. Look at what they've done here: They've conquered an entire nation. They're like what's his name. The Spanish guy who took down the Old-World Incas with two hundred men."

"She's going to kill Christopher," April said.

"We don't know that," Jalil said. "They're not black widows or praying mantises; they don't instantly kill their mates."

"Do they?" David asked me.

I shook my head. "This isn't some little male sex fantasy," I said wearily. "It's about reproduction. Pretty Little Flower thought Christopher made good breeding stock. She'll wait to see if she's pregnant. . . . Then she'll kill him."

"Charming ladies," Jalil muttered. Then he looked at me. "It's kind of up to you, isn't it Senna? We can't fight the Amazons head on. They have Christopher anyway and we can't leave him. We still need your mom to help us with the Coo-Hatch. And only you can get out of here."

David and April both looked sharply at me.

"Yes, I can use my abilities to leave this building," I said. "But I can't change my mother's mind, and I can't somehow beat the Amazons."

"Sobek," Jalil said.

I just stared. I had no reaction prepared. How could Jalil know?

"He's out there still, isn't he?" Jalil said. "Out in the river. And he's still alive and active, unlike Isis and the others here. They sentenced Sobek to lose his priests, to be cut off. And as a result he's the only one still functional."

"Yeah," I admitted. "Yes, Sobek is out there. I don't know why, or what he's waiting for. Maybe he expects Isis to dust off her cobwebs and invite him in. Even if I reach him, what do I ask him to do?"

David and Jalil looked at each other as if hoping the other had the answer. Then David said, "Okay, we want your mom alive and in our hands. We want out of here ourselves. Those are our goals. Period. We have to keep this simple. Senna, get to Sobek if you can. Tell him what the Amazons are doing here. Try to make a deal for us and your mom. If Sobek comes, when he comes, we run for the river. There are still boats down there. I mean blue watercraft. We get out on the water and haul ass for Greece."

"What about Christopher?" April asked.

"No one gets left behind," David said. "If the product hits the fan she'll leave him and come running. One of us —"

"I'll do it," April interrupted. "The Amazons won't expect trouble from me."

I barked a laugh. "You? You're going to take on Pretty Little Flower? With what? Your backpack?"

"No. My voice," April said. "I know some songs your mom can't have taught her."

David nodded as if that made perfect sense. Then he turned to me. "Senna? If you can get us out of here, it'll go a long way to changing how we all look at you."

Unbelievable. As if his opinion, or the cow's opinion, or that smug bastard Jalil's opinion mattered. As if I had to justify myself to them.

I smothered the laugh, kept the derisive grin off my face. And in a parody of his own sincerity, said, "I'll take care of it."

Nothing they said or thought mattered to me.

Still, I'd show them. I would show them.

Chapter XIX

Shape-shifting is relatively easy within Everworld. It is tiring, as all magic is, it requires focus and energy, but it is nothing like the effort required to change a mind or move a physical object.

I'd been doing it since I was a little girl.

The first time was when I was about eight. I'd been with my "new family" for a year. We were all very jolly. All very friendly. "Love, love, love, all you need is love" and all of that. I was just like April.

Except for the fact that I wasn't, of course. Not in my mind, not in anyone's mind. My brand-new mommy and daddy put on a good show, but April was inside the bubble and I was outside.

My stepmother would read to her at night before she went to bed. Not to me. The excuse was that they'd always done it. It was an established ritual. Besides, I never seemed to want to read with her.

So they would curl up in there, in April's room, with just the night-table lamp burning, and the comforter crunched up around them, such a homey little scene. And they would read a chapter of whatever. *Charlotte's Web. Alice in Wonderland. Little Women. The Hobbit.*

It was while they were reading *The Hobbit,* and I was listening through the bathroom door with the light off, crouching there like a thief afraid of being caught, feet cold on the tile, my stupid little blanket clutched in my hands, listening, that I, for the first time, became caught up in the book. *Little Women* had been insipid, *Anne of Green Gables* worse still. But *The Hobbit* reached me in some way.

And I sat there, night after night, listening like I had never done before. Bilbo, the dwarves, the goblins. Gollum. I identified with Gollum, somehow. The first child in history to think Gollum was the hero, sad as he was, alone as he was, desperate and cut off and abandoned as he was. He was one of a kind, Gollum was. A species of one.

There was a stainless-steel trash can in the bathroom, right down near where I sat. And a bar of light from beneath the door. And as I thought about Gollum, and could picture him so clearly, see his condition, see his dank, dark cave . . . I glanced at the trash can. At my bent and distorted reflection.

I stood up! The mirror. Had to see if it was true, couldn't be true. I turned on the light. No, just me. Just my own face staring back at me.

And yet, wait, wait, think about Gollum, remember the words, remember the feeling, and, oh! Oh, oh, oh, impossible! Impossible. I touched my face. Touched my gray, pallid face with webbed hands.

Possible. I was Gollum. The Gollum in my mind, anyway.

That night, after April had kissed her mommy good night and turned off the light, and fallen to sleep with her pretty red curls all laid out on her soft pillow, I went into her room.

I focused my mind again. I drew the glow around me. And I said, "Wake up, my precioussss. Is it awake? Gollum . . . Gollum . . . Or is it dreaming, precioussss?"

A memory I will always treasure. The big, innocent green eyes fluttering open. The scream that penetrated every wall and floor of the house. The scream that would not stop.

It took both her parents an hour to get her back to sleep.

On the down side, I had to read the rest of *The Hobbit* on my own. The nighttime reading switched back to safer ground. But April's nights would never be entirely safe. The Red Queen showed up a few weeks later, looking for heads to chop.

It took me years to really perfect the art. Years before I could do what I did now easily.

I opened the door of the house. Merope, groggy, disgruntled, turned to look. And saw a rat go scurrying out into the night.

"We don't like rats," Jalil explained, and closed the door behind me.

Once out of sight of Merope I dropped that illusion and adopted another — a city full of cats was a bad place for a rat. Now I was my mother. I liked that. She was known to be close to Pretty Little Flower. No one would bother her.

I walked through the dead-silent streets, past the dark temples, a ghost town. Walked down to the river. There was no one on the quay. No guard posted, no one. Two larger and one smaller boat rocked gently.

I resumed my normal appearance, bent over, and stuck my finger in the water that lapped against the stone.

I repeated the tiresome formula for addressing

Sobek and then added, "I humbly request an audience. I have useful information."

I didn't have to wait long. A crocodile's head, too large to be real, too stylized to be a product of nature, rose from the inky water.

"The witch," he hissed.

"Yes. The witch. I kept my bargain: The dam is gone. The Nile flows free again."

"But still great Isis does not call to me," he complained. "I dare not leave the river until I am sure her wrath has cooled."

"Don't worry about Isis. Isis is dead. Or the next best thing. They're all . . . dead but not entirely dead. Your gods don't run this city anymore, Sobek. Strangers have taken over while your fellow gods did nothing. Strangers are emptying all the gold from the city, they are stripping this land bare."

"What lies are these?"

"It's up to you to retake your city. It's up to you to awaken the gods. . . . Unless, of course, you'd rather let them sleep. Then you would be the only god in Egypt."

"The only . . . Sobek the only . . ."

It's a wonderful thing, the lust for power. You can rely on it. Sobek was a minor god, a sort of local god. Like being the governor of Delaware or

Nebraska, I guess. And now he was being offered the White House.

"The Amazons rule this city and this land," I pressed. "They are women warriors, fearsome and strong. They defile the temples, they take everything! There will be nothing left, nothing for you, Sobek. Nothing."

"This cannot be!"

"Then you must stop them. Kill the Amazons, Sobek. You're a god. You could be a great god. You could be the only god in Egypt."

"What must I do?" he whispered, his yellow reptile eyes wide, shining.

"Gather your children," I said. "Take what is rightfully yours. Only leave my companions alone. We will leave this place and leave you to rule as you will."

He did not answer. He didn't have to.

I turned back, my brain going feverishly. How best to exploit this? How best to use the panic that would soon grip this moribund city?

What to do about my mother, that was the question. What to do about —

I turned a corner and stopped dead. She was there. My mother. Standing in the middle of the road — how had she known I would be here, what was she doing? Something. I could see that. Something. A trap? Were Pretty Little Flower's archers all waiting with arrows fitted and bowstrings drawn back, was I already dead and didn't know it?

"Mother?" I asked, shaky, unsure.

"Senda. I . . . I want to do what's best for everyone."

"What have you done?"

"I know I haven't been a good mother. It's too late for that. I mean, I tried, you know? I did. But I have to think about what's good for all of us, you know?"

"What do you want, Mother? What are you talking about?"

"As long as you're free, they'll never stop, they'll never give up. You know that. You know that. Loki . . . Ka Anor . . . That can't happen, it would mess up everything. As long as you're free —"

"What the hell did you do?" I screamed.

Then I felt it. Felt it as if someone had turned on a spotlight behind me, the warm glow, the vibrating power of him. The sure, easy, confident way he drew the power into himself — I could feel it all before I ever saw him, before his name rose bubbling into my consciousness.

"Merlin," I whispered.

Merlin. My mother had sold me out to Merlin. She had summoned him here and now I was alone, facing one like myself, but one with a thousand times more experience.

I froze. I didn't know what to do, couldn't even, the thought had never . . . Merlin. I wanted to attack him but of course I would fail, wanted to run, but no, I was alone, the others all back under guard.

I stood there, staring at my mother, seeing the guilt, seeing the fleeting rush of pleasure, her realization that she had me, had me good. She was sorry, she was glad, she was anxious, she was relieved, she was triumphant. That's what galled me, she was triumphant.

She was giving me to Merlin, like she'd given me to my father: "Here, you take her, she's in my way, she's complicating my life, get her away from me, take her away, lock her up in a life she'll never be able to stand, a life she'll . . ."

My throat was tight. Oh, by all gods, no, not tears. I couldn't cry. I couldn't let my face dissolve into some hideous mask of grief. I couldn't let myself fall apart.

"Come, Senna Wales," Merlin said. Compassion was in his voice. Of course, why not? He could afford compassion, he'd won.

"Where are we going?" I whispered.

"A safe place," he said. "You'll be safe. You will have all you want."

"Hardly," I said harshly.

I turned at last to face him, glad at least not to have to look at my mother's self-pitying, gloating face.

He's an average-sized man, maybe a little smaller. He has a huge gray-white beard and a deeply wrinkled face. Sharp, clear, predatory blue eyes. He wore a mud-splattered dark blue robe and on this occasion a battered slouch hat, almost a 1950s-looking thing. Aside from the hat, he was the picture-perfect wizard. The wizard all the others have been modeled on.

"You've done well to make it this far," he said. "But it's a fool of a mortal who plays games with the gods."

"You play those games," I said.

He smiled. "I invented those games. Come with me. I was carried here by a dragon of my acquaintance. He will carry us both away from here."

"You'll be okay, honey," my mother said. "This is for the best."

Then a new voice. "Hey, what's up? No way, Merlin? What are you doing here?"

Christopher!

I don't know what Merlin thought Christopher would do; I don't know what my mother thought. I knew he'd do nothing. I knew he'd smirk and wish Merlin well. But the point was that neither of them knew that.

"Christopher! Kill my mother!"

"No!" my mother gasped.

And I drew into myself every ounce of power I could and reached to Christopher, touched his mind with an unseen hand, and he lurched. No more, just a lurch, an involuntary reaction, a spasm.

Merlin counterattacked. He raised one bony hand and I could feel the wave of power that flowed from him. He glowed like no mortal ever glowed. Greater by far than my mother. Greater, yes, than me.

And yet I had my opening, slight as it was.

"Amazons! Amazons! Your queen's consort is being murdered! Amazons!"

I saw amazement and confusion on Merlin's face. He didn't know. My mother hadn't told him, and the old man didn't know that the Amazons ruled Egypt now.

"Pretty Little Flower!" I yelled at the top of my lungs. "Your witch has betrayed you!"

Christopher remained frozen in the wizard's spell, and still Merlin did not realize that he was wasting his powers. He didn't know that Christopher was harmless. He held him frozen as a statue while I cried in the night, my voice echoing down the graveyard avenues.

I heard a door slam open. A blur of torches. Shouting female voices. The clatter of weapons. I broke and ran.

Merlin was on me in a flash — he could move far faster than an old man should be able to move. He caught me, grabbed me, spun me around. Christopher was forgotten. My mother was running, scurrying away to find Pretty Little Flower and explain herself, explain the mess she'd made.

Merope arrived in a breathless rush, sword drawn, two other Amazon warriors behind her.

"What is this?" she demanded.

I stabbed a finger at Merlin. "This old man tried to kill your queen's consort and rape me."

"Did he?" Merope roared. "Then I'll send his carcass to Hades!"

Merlin released his physical grip on me. The compassion was gone from his face. He turned his energies against Merope and froze her in mid-attack, froze her with her sword raised over his head.

"You're a great wizard, old man. How many can you hold and still hold me?" I snarled.

I turned, he no longer held my arm with steel-vise fingers, but I could not walk away; my feet were glued to the dust. Merlin's spell held the other two Amazons as they in turn attacked. All of us frozen.

"What the hell is going on here?" Christopher demanded.

"Christopher, take his sword, he can't stop you," I ordered.

"I don't think so," Christopher said, but too late, Merlin had already reacted and now Christopher was immobilized again.

It was time to test my strength against that of the wizard. I drew all I could, all my strength, and tried to step away.

And still, my foot would not budge. Still the

wizard held me, held the five of us with the force of his magic.

"You have much to learn, Senna," he said. In a different voice, not a yell, but a voice intended for other ears, he said, "Come Grymhaldrad. Come to Merlin and fulfill your contract."

The dragon. He was calling the dragon.

More footsteps, more people running. Soon others would arrive, maybe my companions, maybe Pretty Little Flower herself. But if the dragon came, Merlin would have me away from the city before I could hope to stop him.

I had to get away. I needed time. Just a few minutes, no more, just minutes and now, somewhere close by, the dragon was taking wing and still I couldn't move, couldn't budge.

A rush of feet, boots on dirt.

"What have you done to my cuddle lamb?" Pretty Little Flower yelled. "Release him!"

The words *cuddle lamb* threw me off-stride for a moment. They didn't belong, they made no sense. Christopher looked sheepish. Pretty Little Flower stomped over to him, grabbed his arm, and yanked him to her side. He moved like the Tin Man in *The Wizard of Oz*. He still could not control his own limbs.

"I said, let him go, wizard," she seethed.

"This is an affair of magic, Pretty Little Flower. This is not your battle," Merlin warned.

"Bows!" Pretty Little Flower ordered.

Twelve Amazons took all of a half second to fit arrows to their bowstrings and draw those bowstrings tight. Twelve arrows aimed at Merlin's heart.

"Let him go, old meddler. This is my land now. These are my warriors, and he is my cuddle lamb."

The wizard was fighting a losing battle and he knew it. But then, with a rush of air like a tornado, a dragon flew above the roof of Isis' temple and swept above us. Quart droplets of liquid fire dribbled and fell around us.

"I take the witch with me!" Merlin yelled to be heard above the wind and roar of the dragon. "Or Grymhaldrad will fight at my side. How many of your warriors will survive a battle with a dragon? We will have a battle that can profit no one. A battle in which many may die, and much treasure be lost."

If Pretty Little Flower had been a Viking, that would have been an irresistible invitation to slaughter. But the Amazons were not Vikings. The Amazons did not worship glorious death in battle, they worshipped profit and power and survival.

I could see that the Amazon queen was ready to deal, and I would lose. But I could see one thing more: Merlin was tiring. I moved my foot, only an inch, only a little. I moved my eyes, located the nearest darkened doorway, calculated the time it would take.

I was a chess player. But I was my own queen. I risked my own life on the board.

If I moved . . . Merlin would train his powers on me . . . Would he release Merope? Would she strike? Would Pretty Little Flower overreact? Would the dragon . . .

Too many pieces, too many possible moves, too many variables.

No. Wait. There was a move. One winning move.

I tried to still my hammering heart, tried to cleanse all the tumult of emotion from my mind. Forced myself to focus, to allow all that was in me to rise, to narrow, to harden, to sharpen, to . . .

I aimed every ounce of my will at Pretty Little Flower. Not to make her move, not to make her obey, only to make her —

"Ahhh!" she cried in pain, grabbing her stomach.

Twelve arrows flew!

Twelve arrows stopped in midair! Stopped. Hung there quivering.

I broke and ran. Raced, feet flying, all the magic, all the wizardry, it came down to this, to running and hoping. Running and hoping. Up the steps, slam into an unseen pillar, shake it off, woozy, run, run.

Through the door, grab it, too big, too dusty and old, it wouldn't move. A flash of fire that lit up the night! The dragon's fire lit the door, but his fire was not for me, only his light. I saw the stone that held the door ajar. I slid it away and grabbed the door and swung as Merlin bounded up the steps behind me.

Swung the door, slammed it shut in his face, a lock? Surely there was a lock?

A bar, a slide that could be pushed and yes, locked!

Okay, Senna, breathe, breathe. Okay, the door won't hold him, not for long, do it now. So tired, so tired, forget tired! You're not tired, if you're tired you'll live out your life in Merlin's cage.

Not tired. My body was here, trapped, unable to escape, but I had other means. Cross over, Senna. You can't get your body out, but your mind can save you, your powers can save you. You're the gateway, Senna, cross over.

I was suddenly aware that I was not alone. Seated on a stone throne was a god. He had a human body and the head of a ram, with golden horns twisted and spread wide. There were no priests or acolytes. At least none living. Before the altar was a pile of decayed rags that half-covered dessicated corpses. The god himself, whoever he was, was covered with dust and cobwebs.

Don't look. Don't think about it. Not my problem.

I stilled my feverish mind. I drew the powers to me and released my attachment to my physical body. I drifted up and out. Saw through walls, saw the bubble of Everworld stretched beneath me. Merlin was outside the door of the temple. He was trying magic to break open the door, but the door was under the dusty god's protective spell. So Merlin called to his dragon. They would burn through in a minute or two; I had no time. No time.

I flew, disembodied, across the void. The watcher saw me. The watcher noted my fear, my desperation. He/she/it saw me, he/she/it remained unseen by me. Not my problem, not right now. Now my problem was to find someone, some particular someone and fast, fast!

I skimmed above the membrane of the real world, saw the smeared, distorted lens of that reality. Where were my followers? Here and there and nowhere. They were not assembled, of course not. I couldn't find them! Too many minds, too many possibilities, everywhere, a jumble, a swirling mess of minds and bodies and nowhere one of mine that I could find and reach. I needed . . . I needed . . .

There!

Yes, that one. The new one.

Steady, Senna. Steady, Senda the pathway, the gateway, the uniter of universes, it all comes down to this, to here, to now.

I glowed, glowed as never before, forget Merlin's power, forget the gods, I had a different power they couldn't guess at.

I formed the image of the man, the image of the Great One. The god I had invented for fools like this.

Keith sat in his room, a small room, cramped and overheated and dark. He had a bed on the floor, a desk with a computer, screen glowing, AOL account active. He sat, typing furiously. A chat room of some sort.

A swastika poster and a Confederate flag hung on his walls, thumbtacked into faded wallpaper. A stack of bodybuilding magazines with covers of tanned, beefy, oiled men and women. A military footlocker, padlocked.

I appeared in the air behind him. He turned, eyes wide, jerked involuntarily toward the footlocker.

"What the —"

"Are you ready, Keith? Are you ready to answer the call?" I asked, moving an illusion of a mouth, causing an illusion of sound, a deep, resonant, insistent voice.

"How did you get in here?"

"You will address me as Great One!" I roared. This idiot was wasting my time, I had no time, my body was trapped in a room waiting for Merlin's foul, gold-hungry, mercenary beast to burn me out.

Keith blinked. A slight nod. He glanced around the room, embarrassed by what I was seeing. "What do you want?" Pause. "Great One?"

"You, Keith. You. And all the weapons in that footlocker."

He froze. Guarded. Scared. Unsure. Tempted.

"Now or never," I said, trying not to sound desperate. "Now or never. Do you want to stand at my right hand? Do you want to sit in this squalid room forever, or do you want to pursue your destiny? Will you grab your destiny with both hands?"

Hesitation. Ticktock. The dragon, how long did I have till he burned his way through?

Keith knelt and spun the combination lock on the footlocker. He threw back the lid. How many guns? Three at least, and steel boxes of ammunition, long gray clips loaded. Keith grabbed, stuffed ammunition and clips into his pockets, his shirt, his belt. Two guns, a handgun and something still deadlier. The weight was almost too much for him, but weight didn't matter to me.

I turned my attention inward, collapsed myself into myself. I drew my body to my mind, my mind to my body, unified myself, drew all of me together.

I opened the gateway.

In a flash, in an instant it was open. I was open. I was a tunnel between universes, my body hollow, my mind seeing, feeling both worlds at the same instant, and more worlds besides.

Glorious! A rush, an incredible rush. A heroin addict's rush of drugs into his blood, a drunk's first drink burning down a raw, ready throat. Oh, oh, I wanted to, to scream, to flail out of control. It was mind, it was body, it was sex and money and power and revenge and triumph all rolled into one.

I was in Keith's room and in the temple, and they were no longer two places but one. A Confederate flag hung on the wall of the dusty goat god's temple. A computer screen bathed the crumpled bones of his priests with a blue glow.

But I was also in the spaceless space between universes. I felt the watcher's eye on me, but oh, so many more eyes, too. The gods felt me, became aware of me, some only vaguely, some felt a mere disturbance, but others snapped their gaze toward me in a flash and knew exactly, exactly what had happened.

I felt Loki's malevolent outrage, felt Ka Anor's

surprise, and others without name, all seeing me, knowing that the gateway was open, that the wall between universes had become an open door.

I snapped the door shut, cascaded back into Everworld, and there I was again, within myself, trembling, a thin-faced girl, exhausted, kneeling near a door that blazed yellow and red in the darkness. The heat was like a blast furnace. In a second the door would melt into a puddle or burst into flame.

Keith stared, wild-eyed, uncomprehending.

I stood, grabbed his arm, my own true self now, no male god figure. "It's me you work for," I snapped. "You want power, I'll give it to you. You want to live, I'll save you. Me and no one else."

"Who the hell are you?" he demanded.

"There's a dragon on the other side of that door. He'll be in here very soon. Shoot him. And shoot the old man with him."

All at once the door melted. Stone had been turned to magma. Liquid stone puddled.

The fire was quenched. Through the smoke and cinders a dragon's arrogant head, mouth dribbling napalm, was thrust into the room.

The beast eyed Keith. Saw me. Said, "Well, Master Merlin, there will have to be an extra charge for burning down that door. Enchanted doors are very hard to burn."

I put my hand on Keith's shoulder, touched him, reached into his murderous mind and pushed him the little bit he needed to be pushed.

The submachine gun erupted. The noise was deafening. Spent brass shells clattered on the stone floor.

Bullets tore into the dragon's head. How many, I don't know. It was all too fast, all too sudden. I felt the vibration of the recoil.

The dragon looked surprised. Hurt. As though his feelings were hurt, as though . . .

He fell suddenly. Like a marionette with the strings sliced. The massive head simply crashed to the floor. The liquid fire in his mouth spilled out. Keith jumped aside to avoid it, I scurried back.

"The old man," I snapped. "Where is he? Get the old man! Go!"

But Keith didn't even hear me. He let out a shrill yell of triumph and pranced in front of the dead dragon. "Aha! I killed it! I killed it! Did you see that? I freakin' killed it! Ba-boom."

He was nearly hysterical, out of control. The ram god must have stirred slightly and Keith heard the noise. He spun, leveled his weapon from the waist and fired again.

I pushed past the dragon, ran from the temple. Keith was insane, killing anything. I might be next. Had to take my chances outside.

Where was Merlin?

In the street, madness. Sheer madness. A seething river of crocodiles washed down the street, sinuous, slithering, twisting reptiles by the hundreds.

The Amazons were atop stone monuments, scattered, firing arrows down into the crocodiles. Arrow after arrow found its mark. Crocodiles died and their fellows crawled over their corpses.

I froze, stared, unable to take it all in. It was as horrifying as anything I'd seen since Hel's underworld. Slaughter. Mayhem.

The crocodiles were a rioting mob. Just in front of me half a dozen of the beasts were tearing apart the body of a priest. The Amazons kept up a disciplined fire, killing and killing, but never slowing the invasion.

Where was Merlin? Where were the others? And my mother? No one in sight. Just crocodiles surging up stairways, looking to cut off and surround the viragos.

The temple of Isis. If the others were anywhere, if my mother was anywhere, it would be there.

But how to reach it? How to cross a street filled with murder?

Behind me, from within the temple, came the muted sound of gunshots. What was the sick little creep up to now? I had to get away. Merlin,

Keith, the crocodiles, the Amazons, dangers on all sides.

Then came Sobek. He had grown to massive size. He strode down the street, twenty feet tall, the stylized crocodile head looming, a nightmare dinosaur.

He stepped on the backs of his children, indifferent to them. Straight toward the nearest knot of Amazons. Pretty Little Flower was among them.

"Forget the crocodiles!" she yelled.

The Amazons shifted their aim and began pouring arrows into the god. Three, seven, fifteen arrows sprouted from his crocodile head. Sobek laughed and swept the shafts away.

"Do you attack a god?" he demanded.

Pretty Little Flower never flinched. She reached for her Coo-Hatch throwing blade. The Coo-Hatch blade that would cut anything. Huitzilopoctli had been injured by an enchanted hammer. Could Sobek be hurt by a Coo-Hatch blade? Gods were immortal, not invulnerable.

One chance.

"Sobek!" I yelled. "Beware! She has an enchanted blade!"

Pretty Little Flower shot me a murderous look. Then she let fly with the Coo-Hatch blade. Too late. Sobek jerked aside, the blade passed harmlessly and circled back toward Pretty Little Flower. She was no longer there to retrieve it.

Sobek had opened his mouth and darted in to grab Pretty Little Flower. He snatched her off her pedestal, shook her like a dog shaking a rat, and tossed her to the crocodiles.

The Amazons stayed strong. But they knew it was time to retreat. Egypt was theirs no longer. They formed into a hollow square and backed toward the nearest open door. Their arrows were spent. They fought with swords and daggers against the crocodiles.

Sobek watched for a while, satisfied. Then he turned his evil yellow eyes on me. "I was wise to spare you. What is your wish?"

"I must reach the temple of Isis."

"Then reach it you will." He lifted me up and placed me on his shoulder. I was Fay Wray atop King Kong. He marched down the avenue, carried me above the slaughter, and deposited me safely on the steps of Isis' temple.

"Egypt is mine," Sobek said. "You and yours will be gone from this city before the sun reaches noon tomorrow. After that, you, too, will die. Thus speaks Sobek, lord of all Egypt!"

"We'll be gone," I said.

I dragged myself, shattered, up the steps and collapsed into David's arms. He was waiting, sword drawn, face grim.

He hauled me roughly into the temple and Christopher pushed the door shut behind us. The sudden silence was unnerving. The screams, the hisses and roars, all shut out.

"Merlin?" I gasped. "Is he here?"

"No. Christopher said he was around. Said your mom sold you out."

I nodded. Had to gather my wits, had to get it together. Had to get control. But I was empty. Beat and confused. None of it was according to plan. Nothing made sense. Madness and betrayal and violence.

"Pretty Little Flower is dead," I managed. "The Amazons are done for. Sobek has the city. We have till noon tomorrow."

"Don't worry, we'll get out of this hellhole just as fast as we can," April said. Her face was tear-streaked, dirty. No, not dirty, bloody.

"She's dead?" Christopher said.

For a minute I couldn't figure out what he was asking. "Pretty Little Flower? Yes, I'd say she's dead."

He nodded. "She was okay."

"She was a killer, you imbecile," I snapped. "She'd have killed you eventually. No matter how good you think you are."

"It wasn't like that," he insisted. "We didn't do it. We just . . . you know. We cuddled."

Was I losing my mind? Was I in some absurd dream? What was the fool talking about? We were surrounded by crocodiles who were busily killing anything that moved. And he was moping for Pretty Little Flower?

"We have your mom," David said.

That reenergized me. "Where?" I snarled. "Show me where she is." I got up, swept the hair out of my face, and started to go in search of her.

David stopped me, held me back with one hand. I could have made him eat his own hand given enough energy, but as it was, all I could do was scream.

"She sold me out to Merlin! She sold me out again. Again! I'll destroy her."

David nodded. "She knows."

Jalil appeared for the first time, stepping out of the gloom. "She's scared of you. Doesn't know what you'll do to her. We made a deal."

"A deal?" I asked stupidly.

"Yes. A deal. She takes care of the Coo-Hatch. She will become a gateway and help them to escape. But she wants something in return."

"To live?" I grated.

"To be forgiven," Jalil said.

I laughed. I laughed and didn't think I could

stop. She what? She what? She wanted forgiveness?

"You mean she wants to know she's safe from me," I said.

David nodded. "Yes. That's the deal. She does the Coo-Hatch, once she's in a safe place, that is. That will take a while. But once she gets away from here and finds a safe place for herself, she'll help the Coo-Hatch. Only not if she's looking over her shoulder waiting for you."

Jalil said, "She knows she wasn't a very good mother. She knows that. She's so sorry. She's sorry about everything. Maybe she was weak, maybe you were right, all the things you said. But she never meant to . . ." Jalil sobbed.

David's gaze never flickered.

I shook my head, not sure whether to laugh or cry. Jalil sobbing. Right.

My mother the shape-shifter.

What was I supposed to do? She had abandoned me once, and given me over to Merlin. What was I supposed to do?

"You underestimated me," I said softly to Jalil-who-was-not-Jalil. "You could have been with me. You went to Isis, you went to Pretty Little Flower, you went to Merlin. And all the time, Mother, all the time, I was the one who could have saved you. Everworld will be mine, Mother. Mine."

"Please . . . I'm not . . . Please . . ." Jalil said. "Despite everything, I am your mother."

The image of Jalil began to soften, shrink, to slide toward the image of a woman I'd never known, a million years ago. I saw the real Jalil now standing discreetly off to one side.

"No. Don't change, Mother. Here's my deal: You can escape this city, if you know how. And as long as you take care of the Coo-Hatch and keep your bargain, you won't have me to fear. But I'll never see your face again."

"I could still be good for you," she said. "I still could teach you, show you how . . ."

I turned my back, slowly, deliberately. Turned away. Left her to stand there pleading helplessly.

And it should have been so sweet. It should have been a perfect moment. It should have been vindication for the little girl who had wondered night after night why her mother had . . .

It should have been so sweet.

Instead I felt hollow. Like my insides had all been carved out.

Well, I was tired, that was it. Tired. It's exhausting being me.

#X

Understand the Unknown

It was a smaller boat than ours, and faster. Maybe it was bringing up the wind, riding at the front of a new breeze, but I didn't believe it. Not from that direction, not running exactly counter to our own breeze. No. That boat was self-propelled somehow. There were no engines in Everworld, the place was not about technology, so whoever was in that boat was commanding the wind to rise just for him.

I looked at Senna. She was alert. Watching. Her gray eyes were dark with worry, the color of mercury.

"It's him," she said. "It's Merlin."

"Yeah. That was my guess, too."

We had evaded the old man in Egypt. He'd been called there by Senna's mother but in the chaos of destruction that had followed we'd lost him.

As the strange boat closed in on us I could see the old man's long, once-blond, now grayish hair and beard, imagine his intelligent blue eyes, sunken beneath a lined brow. Remember what I'd seen him do, bring dead animals to life, make a wall rise from a pile of rubble, command a dragon to do his bidding, hold fierce Amazon warriors in suspension.

This was the wizard who wanted Senna, who wanted to keep her from Loki's clutches. Who would imprison her if he could, kill her if he had to.

Wasn't going to happen. Not if I could help it.

"Everyone up," I said. "We have trouble."

Jalil, Christopher, and April stirred, awoke with varying degrees of grace.

Christopher shaded his eyes and stared. "It's freaking Merlin, man."

I called to Nikos. The captain was sitting in the shade under an awning, drinking wine with what had to be the first officer, a guy who occasionally stirred himself to yell at the rowers. The two of them were moderately drunk, but the sight of that sail sobered them pretty quickly.

"Captain? Can we outrun him?" Knew that it was a ridiculous question. How would the captain know the extent of Merlin's magic?

Nikos knew as well as I did that the other boat was not obeying the usual laws of sailing. "The gods will decide," he said with a fatalistic shrug.

"Well kick the rowers into high gear," I said. "And raise sail. We may get close enough to ram him."

"This is my ship, friend," Nikos said. "I will decide. And I do not wish to offend the gods. No. That boat is too small to be a pirate, he cannot attempt to board and take us. I think he is interested in something else." He gave me a fish-eyed look that made clear he was not risking his ship for our sakes. The gods wanted us badly enough to blow this boat toward us? Fine with him, he'd been paid, and the gods were welcome to us. No point in threatening a fight: the crew was small for a ship this size, but Nikos still had sixty guys.

"You worry about the gods? This isn't about the gods. See her?" I pointed at Senna. "She's a witch. Raise sail or she turns your cargo to so much worm food."

The captain thought that over for a moment. There's a real shortage of skepticism in Everworld and he never doubted my word that Senna was a witch.

"Raise the sail," Nikos ordered. "We will run before the wind, but we will not outrun the will of the gods."

That was the extent of my brilliant plan. Raise

sail and hope our fitful breeze would carry us away from Merlin's purposeful wind.

The rowers advanced their rhythm, the sail dropped, and we turned to take the wind from straight aft. The ship responded. I could feel it surge forward and I could see that it didn't make a damned bit of difference. The other boat would catch us. And then what? Was it Merlin alone? If so maybe we could still keep him from boarding.

Then again, maybe not.

Didn't want to ask the others for ideas, though if someone made a brilliant suggestion, I'd put the plan in motion. Better Jalil's plan, or Christopher's, than no plan at all. No plan was what I had.

Senna? No. She had powers, but she was like a really good high school player trying to go one-on-one with Shaq. She was a long way from taking Merlin down.

What were we going to —

The sea erupted! The stretch of sea separating the two converging boats simply erupted, a pillar of water billowed and rose up, impossible.

It looked like some sort of bizarre Hollywood special effect. The sea was opening up, rising up, forming a twisting pillar of boiling green water. It looked like . . .

"It's like the Ten freaking Commandments!" Christopher yelled. Exactly. Like the movie when the Israelites cross the Red Sea. But now the water was taking shape. A huge figure was emerging from the swirling green whirlpool. It undulated wildly, but still a vague outline was discernible. A man, a human, at least a creature vaguely resembling a human.

A god. Had to be.

Like a massive, shifting, crudely human-shaped jellyfish. Translucent, like a giant blob of hair gel on the palm of the water, piled upon the water, rising from it.

And inside the creature, part of the creature, swimming around in its belly and brain, there were what looked a hell of a lot like dolphins and sharks and rays and other sea creatures I couldn't quite make out. Clumps of seaweed for all I knew. Maybe whales, it was big enough.

The crew moaning and praying and wailing, the name "Poseidon" on every tongue.

April, making the sign of the cross. Jalil, open-mouthed, still in some way, on some level outraged by the mere fact of magic, the Everworld reality of charms, spells, physical laws broken and mended and broken again. Christopher trembling, mumbling something about Charlton Heston, Pharoah, and let my freaking people go.

Senna, standing alone, facing the monstrosity, a cold wind making her hair blow straight back. Calculating. Wondering whether this was Merlin's doing or whether the sailors were right and this was some far greater power.

And then, the watery thing spoke.

The voice, if that's what it was; hard to tell with my eardrums near to bursting and my eyes closing against the sound, my feet slipping out from under me, knees hitting the wooden deck. The voice spoke, shouted, roared like a too, too loud surround sound system in a too, too small movie theatre. The voice seemed to come from the entire body of living water, from no one place in particular, no lips moving or tongue wagging.

"Who dares to command the winds and waters of mighty Neptune? Who dares use magic to challenge my will?"

It took me a second to get it. Neptune wasn't pissed at us. He was after Merlin!

I saw Merlin doing a quick bow-and-scrape and looking more nervous than I'd have thought possible.

"This arrogance, this impudence will not go unpunished," Neptune roared.

Then . . . he, it, Neptune was gone.

The squall attacked with such sudden violence it was like the concussion of a bomb. Wind of terrifying, irresistable force. The squall hit the sail, laid us over on our side. I slid, fell, tumbled down a deck as suddenly as pitched as an IHOP roof. I hit the rail, slammed hard, arm numbed.

A wall of green water swept over the ship. Would we come up? Would the boat swim?

The wave swept past, carrying away the mast, the sail, oars, many of the rowers, and all the crates and crap that had been stowed carelessly around the deck.

The ship began to right itself, but so slowly, so heavily. It wallowed like a barrel. I spit water, clawed my way back to the oar, had to be able to steer, if the next wave caught us broadside we were all done.

"Row!" I bellowed. "Damn it, row!" The only hope was to get the ship moving, get her bow into the waves.

No rowers. The crew that hadn't been washed overboard was in a state of weeping panic.

I saw a soaked, battered Jalil stagger to a surviving oar, but no way, not one guy, wasn't happening and now the second wave, the mother of all waves was bearing down.

The deck fell away sickeningly as we slid into the trough. The wave towered above us, towered above where the mast would have been. It was a mountain of water. No hope.

A hammer blow that caught me, snatched me away from my precarious hold on the steering oar and carried me away, once more to be stopped by the bulwark. I was half drowned, dazed, bruised.

Still she swam. But the quinquireme was low in the water. Gunwales barely clear.

The crew, what was left, clung helplessly to rails and the stump of the mast. So did my friends. Hopeless. Another wave coming. Relentless. If we stayed any longer we'd go down, sucked down with the ship.

"Off the bow!" I yelled in the weird calm between waves. "Grab an oar, jump! Go, go, go!"

I saw April running. Christopher limping. The deck tilted perilously. We were stern on to the wave. Now we were rolling, falling toward the bow.

Christopher jumped. Where was Senna?

The wave . . . I jumped.

The wave lifted the boat nearly vertical, slammed into the stern, and drove the ship down like a spike under a sledgehammer's blow. The ship speared into the water and disappeared.

"Senna!"

Suction caught me, a swirling drain with me no more than a bug. Blinded by saltwater and confusion and pain, I put one hand over my head, palm flat up, and kicked, used my left arm as a paddle, had to get to the surface, hell, I could be on the surface, couldn't tell, woozy, head hurt. Remember, David, save yourself first, be able to save others . . .

Palm hit something hard, better than hitting my head. I felt along the object, lungs beginning to burn, still blind, kicked to my left, used the free arm again to propel myself beyond the barrier, strong stroke down . . . broke free! Air! I took deep, deep breaths, another slap of water almost choked me, rushed down into my lungs. I coughed, gagged, rubbed my eyes until they opened, blink, blink, had to find the others, had to find Senna!

I grabbed a floating timber. All that was left.

"Who's there?!" I shouted, but I didn't know if anyone could hear my voice over the boiling sea, a sea tormented into an artificial frenzy by Neptune, a sea meant to kill us. A sky lowering and black, a sky now raining hailstones like bullets. Impossible to see. The waves were mountains around me. I rose with the swell, was swamped by the crest, slid down the far side of the wave.

Then . . . through the needlelike spray and biting foam, a form, a figure. I kicked, thrust my arms through the water, breast-stroked, dog paddled, anything to fight my way through the chaotic sea, to get closer to that form, that person . . .

"April! April, hold on!"